"You sure my staying won't cause any problems?" Sebastian asked.

"With who?" Stephanie had no idea what he was talking about.

"Your significant other."

"You keep saying that, but there is no significant other."

He studied her, wondering how much she'd changed in the last seven years. "Then it was casual?"

Her patience felt like a wet tissue, about to dissolve. "Was *what* casual?"

Frustration took a second pass at him. "You got pregnant, and as far as I know, there's only been one Immaculate Conception on record."

Stephanie drew herself up, squaring her shoulders. "Yes, but there've been a great many in vitro fertilizations since then."

"In vitro…" He stared at her as his voice trailed away. "Why would you do that?"

"You don't have the right to ask me questions like that anymore."

Dear Reader,

International bestselling author Diana Palmer needs no introduction. Widely known for her sensual and emotional storytelling, and with more than forty million copies of her books in print, she is one of the genre's most treasured authors. And this month, Special Edition is proud to bring you the exciting conclusion to her SOLDIERS OF FORTUNE series. *The Last Mercenary* is the thrilling tale of a mercenary hero risking it all for love. Between the covers is the passion and adventure you've come to expect from Diana Palmer!

Speaking of passion and adventure, don't miss *To Catch a Thief* by Sherryl Woods in which trouble—in the form of attorney Rafe O'Donnell—follows Gina Petrillo home for her high school reunion and sparks fly.... Things are hotter than the Hatfields and McCoys in Laurie Paige's *When I Dream of You*— when heat turns to passion between two families that have been feuding for three generations!

Is a heroine's love strong enough to heal a hero scarred inside and out? Find out in *Another Man's Children* by Christine Flynn. And when an interior designer pretends to be a millionaire's lover, will *Her Secret Affair* lead to a public proposal? Don't miss *An Abundance of Babies* by Marie Ferrarella—in which double the babies and double the love could be just what an estranged couple needs to bring them back together.

This is the last month to enter our Silhouette Makes You a Star contest, so be sure to look inside for details. And as always, enjoy these fantastic stories celebrating life, love and family.

Best,
Karen Taylor Richman
Senior Editor

Please address questions and book requests to:
Silhouette Reader Service
U.S.: 3010 Walden Ave., P.O. Box 1325, Buffalo, NY 14269
Canadian: P.O. Box 609, Fort Erie, Ont. L2A 5X3

An Abundance of Babies

MARIE FERRARELLA

Silhouette®

SPECIAL EDITION™

Published by Silhouette Books

America's Publisher of Contemporary Romance

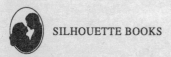 SILHOUETTE BOOKS

ISBN 0-373-24422-3

AN ABUNDANCE OF BABIES

Visit Silhouette at www.eHarlequin.com

Printed in U.S.A.

Books by Marie Ferrarella in Miniseries

ChildFinders, Inc.
A Hero for All Seasons IM #932
A Forever Kind of Hero IM #943
Hero in the Nick of Time IM #956
Hero for Hire IM #1042
An Uncommon Hero Silhouette Books
A Hero in Her Eyes IM #1059

Baby's Choice
Caution: Baby Ahead SR #1007
Mother on the Wing SR #1026
Baby Times Two SR #1037

Baby of the Month Club
Baby's First Christmas SE #997
Happy New Year Baby! IM #686
The 7lb., 2oz. Valentine Yours Truly
Husband: Optional SD #988
Do You Take This Child? SR #1145
Detective Dad World's Most
   Eligible Bachelors
The Once and Future Father IM #1017
In the Family Way Silhouette Books
Baby Talk Silhouette Books
An Abundance of Babies SE #1422

Like Mother, Like Daughter
One Plus One Makes Marriage SR #1328
Never Too Late for Love SR #1351

*The Pendletons
Baby in the Middle SE #892
Husband, Some Assembly Required SE #931

Those Sinclairs
Holding Out for a Hero IM #496
Heroes Great and Small IM #501
Christmas Every Day IM #538
Caitlin's Guardian Angel IM #661

Two Halves of a Whole
The Baby Came C.O.D. SR #1264
Desperately Seeking Twin Yours Truly

The Cutlers of the Shady Lady Ranch
(Yours Truly titles)
Fiona and the Sexy Stranger
Cowboys Are for Loving
Will and the Headstrong Female
The Law and Ginny Marlow
A Match for Morgan

*The Reeds
Callaghan's Way IM #601
Serena McKee's Back in Town IM #808

*McClellans & Marinos
Man Trouble SR #815
The Taming of the Teen SR #839
Babies on His Mind SR #920
The Baby Beneath the Mistletoe SR #1408

*The Alaskans
Wife in the Mail SE #1217
Stand-In Mom SE #1294
Found: His Perfect Wife SE #1310
The M.D. Meets His Match SE #1401

*Unflashed series

MARIE FERRARELLA

earned a master's degree in Shakespearean comedy and, perhaps as a result, her writing is distinguished by humor and natural dialogue. This RITA Award-winning author has one goal: to entertain, to make people laugh and feel good. She has written over a hundred books for Silhouette, some under the name Marie Nicole. Her romances are beloved by fans worldwide and have been translated into Spanish, Italian, German, Russian, Polish, Japanese and Korean.

Chapter One

It had been more than a week and she still couldn't shake free of the feeling that her whole world was crashing in on her.

It was hard to focus, to try to pull herself out of this latest tailspin her life had gone into. Hard to put one foot in front of the other and go on. Though a child of luxury who had never wanted for anything, at least financially, Stephanie Yarbourough was no stranger to the tough curves and hardballs life could, without warning, suddenly throw at her. So far, she'd managed to dodge them all.

First there'd been her mother. Joan Yarbourough had just picked up and disappeared, without so much as a card at Christmas to show that she still remembered she had left behind a daughter as well as a stepson when she'd walked out on her husband. It had taken time, but she'd gotten over that, Stephanie thought. Gotten over being forgotten at eight.

And then there'd been Sebastian. He's disappeared out of her life the summer before she turned twenty-one and she'd gotten over that, too, hadn't she?

Well, maybe not altogether, but at least to the point where she'd become a functioning human being again, able to go on with her life. Anger had helped then. Anger had coated the hurt, the searing, bottomless pain of being summarily rejected without so much as a word of explanation.

But this latest pitch that fate had hurled at her had hit her right between the eyes. After this one she just didn't know if she was going to be able to summon the wherewithal to pull herself together again.

She felt the kick. Or was that kicks? They came in quick succession, like dancers in a syncopated line, as if to remind her that she was never alone.

She had no choice but to pull herself together, Stephanie told herself sternly, feeling her eyes beginning to sting. This wasn't just about her, but about the babies she was carrying. This had happened to them as well as to her.

Maybe even more.

Her mouth curved sadly as she lay her hand protectively over her swollen belly. Holly and Brett's babies.

Except that they were never going to be able to hold them, not now.

Not ever.

"Are you all right, Ms. Yarbourough?"

Blinking, she looked up to see the pharmacist looking at her over the raised counter. There was a touch of concern in his brown eyes.

"What?"

The concern deepened a degree as the old man looked at her more closely. "I said, 'Are you all right, Ms. Yarbourough?' You stopped signing the charge slip and looked as if you were somewhere else miles away from here."

The rueful smile came and went, replaced by a complacent one. Facades had always been part of her world and she had learned her lesson well at her father's knee: never let them know what you're thinking.

Stephanie finished signing the slip and offered it back to the white-haired man.

"I was."

"Hopefully it was some place air-conditioned." Silas Abernathy chuckled, separating the yellow copy from the others and snapping it off. He offered the slip to her. She noticed that a thatch of his hair was pasted to his forehead. "These voluntary brown-outs are a bear."

"A little air is better than none," Stephanie murmured philosophically, absently dropping the charge slip into her purse. Weather, a nice, banal topic, she thought.

A wave of bitterness swept over her the next moment as she snapped her purse shut. Unseasonable heat had been the reason Holly and Brett had decided to go off on an impromptu, three-day vacation. A vacation they'd invited her to share, but, miserably uncomfortable in her condition, she'd opted to remain home.

If she hadn't...

Stephanie shut the thought away. No sense in going there.

"Good attitude," Mr. Abernathy was saying, slipping her prescription into a small, slim bag. "Wish all my customers thought like you did. Can't tell you how many come in here, complaining about the lack of air in the store. As if it was my idea to cut down on the power." He shook his head. "And they're not even in your condition." He held out the bag to her, his eyes on her very swollen belly, a belly no amount of fabric, with its artful folds and layers, could any longer disguise. "Any day now, huh?"

Because the man was as old as her grandfather would have been had he lived, and just as kindly, Stephanie took no offense at the very personal probing, though these last few days, she'd taken offense at almost anything.

"Any day now," she confirmed brightly.

And much, much too soon, she thought, taking the small paper bag with her prenatal vitamins in them.

Extra prenatal vitamins her obstetrician, Sheila Pollack, had prescribed because she was still so dangerously anemic. The babies were taking a lot out of her.

She wasn't ready.

Wasn't ready to greet these babies she'd suddenly been placed in sole charge of. They weren't supposed to be her babies, they were supposed to belong to Brett and Holly. She didn't know if she could love them the way they were meant to be loved.

Holly and Brett had been so eager, so filled with love for them from the very first moment the test had turned positive.

Maybe even before.

Murmuring something that passed for ''goodbye,'' Stephanie turned away from the counter and made her way to the pharmacy's electronic doors, feeling not unlike a lumbering bear.

The doors yawned open as she approached. With the doors no longer acting as a barrier, a blast of heat came at her.

She bit her lower lip as she stepped outside and the southern California heat surrounded her in an atypically hot, sweaty embrace. Even the air she drew into her lungs was heavy, daunting.

It was all supposed to have been so straightforward, so easy. Far less complicated than most surrogate mother arrangements. Her brother, Matthew, a corporate attorney, had insisted on documents being signed, though she'd never felt the need for that.

She'd done this out of love for a woman who had been closer to her than a sister—certainly closer to her than her own father had ever been.

Hell, it had been her idea in the first place.

She'd volunteered to do this over Holly and Brett's initial self-conscious protests. Desperate for a child, the couple still hadn't wanted to put her through this. It had taken more than a little convincing on her part to make them both understand that this was something she was more than willing to do if it meant that they could ultimately have their life's dream come true: a child of their very own.

But "easy" had turned complicated right from the start.

The "child" had turned into "children" shortly after her pregnancy had been confirmed. Sheila had been bubbling with pleasure when she'd told her that she was pregnant not with one baby, but with two. The whole procedure had taken only two tries.

Fertility personified, that was her. But then she already knew that, she thought, fighting a second onslaught of tears. She and Sebastian had shared one time together, just one time, and she'd become pregnant with his child.

A child he'd never even known about. A child she'd lost soon after she'd lost him. It was as if she wasn't allowed to hang on to anything at all that would remind her of his ever having been in her life.

Except for fading memories she couldn't seem to

eradicate from her head no matter how often or how hard she tried.

There was no doubt in her mind that he'd long since purged her from his.

It didn't matter. He wasn't part of her life anymore, hadn't been for seven years. But these babies were.

Her hand went over her belly again. She had two babies on the way and no parents waiting in the wings to receive them.

Damn, why did life have to keep getting this complicated? Why couldn't things go right for a change? Was that asking too much?

Dragging her hair off her neck, she stepped away from the marginal shade cast by the pharmacy's awning and ventured out into the parking lot. She could feel the heat sizzling as it rose up along her legs. The asphalt felt as if it was going to liquefy with very little encouragement.

So, probably, she mused, could she. She'd never responded well to heat, and now, since she'd gotten pregnant, it was twice as bad.

With a sigh, Stephanie looked around, trying to remember where she had parked her car with its life-saving air-conditioning.

Stephanie Yarbourough.

The sight of her struck him with the force of a two-by-four being swung directly at his middle.

She wasn't the last person he'd ever expected to

see here. After all, Bedford was her hometown, just as it had once been his. But he'd never expected to see her like that, her belly clearly distended beneath the wide, blue-and-white floral print dress.

Pregnant.

Stephanie was carrying some other man's child.

And why not? he demanded of himself dourly. She damn well had a right to go on with her life. Wasn't that what it had been all about, his leaving Bedford almost seven years ago? To allow her to go on with her life the way he knew in his heart it was really meant to go on? With someone from her own class. Someone who knew what fork to use, what words to say. Someone she would never find herself being ashamed of, who could make things happen for her the way he couldn't.

Yes, that was what his leaving had been all about, he thought. But in all the time that had passed, he hadn't once considered the possibility of Stephanie giving herself to anyone else.

Wanted to be her one and only, despite all your so-called noble intentions, didn't you, Sebastian? he mocked himself.

But it hadn't been because of some vain desire on his part. It had been because he'd loved her. And wanted to go on loving her. Forever. And he'd wanted her to love him that way.

Showed how naive the tough kid from the wrong side of the tracks had been, Sebastian thought cynically, leaning over the steering wheel of his abruptly halted car to get a better look at her. In the pressed pages of his mind, Stephanie had remained eternally twenty, eternally innocent.

He debated driving on. Just shutting the image he'd just seen out of his mind and moving on, mentally and physically. After all, he hadn't returned to Bedford because he wanted to pick up where he'd left off. He'd returned because he was needed.

Go, damn it, she hasn't seen you. Go.

He didn't listen. Instead, he pulled up the hand brake on the car and turned off the key in the ignition. A force greater than noble thoughts and the need for self-preservation had him getting out of the car close to where she was wandering through the parking lot.

"Stevi?"

Hearing the voice above the din of passing cars and stray voices in the lot, Stephanie froze. Despite the scorching heat, she felt s sharp chill zip like lightning up and down her spine. She told herself that she was hearing things, that she was imagining them.

The way she'd thought and imagined his voice calling to her a hundred times since he'd left.

Only one person in the world called her Stevi. And that person had gone out of her life almost seven years ago.

Her body and limbs suddenly leaden, Stephanie found herself turning stiffly toward the source of the voice—determined to prove to herself that she hadn't heard what she thought she had.

Praying she hadn't.

Praying she had.

Eye contact was made instantly. Stephanie felt her heart stop beating for a second, then slam into her rib cage, accelerating so fast it threatened to make her dizzy.

Like a defense mechanism on a hair trigger, anger sprang up, immediate, full-grown and strong.

Life wasn't fair. Not on any count. Sebastian Caine wasn't supposed to be here, wasn't supposed to be so damn good-looking he could move a portrait of a woman to sigh in abject desire.

His face was leaner, tanner than she remembered. His expression—that "bad boy" look her father had always ranted about—seemed as if it was now permanently chiseled in. Sebastian looked all the more sensually attractive for it.

As if he needed that.

He'd always been sensuality itself, just by breathing, by the way he'd looked at her. By the mere set of his shoulders.

Stephanie stayed where she was, her hands fisted at her sides. Her car, her condition, everything else forgotten but the man who had suddenly materialized in her life without warning.

Just the way he'd disappeared.

If life *had* been fair, Sebastian would have gotten fatter, ugly and been balding, not have dark chestnut hair curling from the humidity at the back of his neck and along his forehead. Hair she'd once dived her fingers through, glorying in the feel of it.

Damn you, Sebastian. Not now. Not after I've gotten over you.

A little voice inside her said, *Ha, sure you've gotten over him,* but she ignored it.

Her feet felt glued to the asphalt. As Sebastian walked toward her, she could almost see each muscle moving independently, yet in harmony, like a jaguar that was stalking its prey.

Except that he had nothing to stalk.

Unless jaguars stalked overly pregnant women, she ridiculed herself. She felt as if she'd gained a thousand pounds within the last two seconds.

What did it matter? He hadn't wanted her when she'd been model-thin and completely willing to give up her world for him, she reminded herself. She'd made it clear she was willing to go anywhere with him, follow him to the ends of the earth. All that had mattered to her was being with him.

But she hadn't mattered enough to him.

Stephanie lifted her chin as the distance between them decreased, searching for something to say even as her eyes swept the parking lot, trying to locate her car for a quick getaway. Why did she always forget where she parked? And why now of all times?

What were the first words out of your mouth when you saw, after seven years, the man who broke your heart and set fire to your dreams? Did you rant? Did you ignore him? What? she thought in utter frustration. Emily Post and her cohorts didn't cover this in their books on proper etiquette.

Maybe because proper ladies didn't get dumped, Stephanie thought ruefully. Proper ladies didn't pour out their hearts and let the man they loved know they loved him. There had been no mystery between Sebastian and her. Except the ultimate one—why he had left.

There it was, her car. One aisle over.

Because it was too far away to reach without passing him, she summoned all the years of training her father had tried to drum into her head—"So that I will never have reason to be ashamed of you"—and pasted a meaningless, distant smile on her face.

"Hello, Sebastian. How are you?"

The frost in her voice hit him like the steep, sleek side of an iceberg. He should have just kept driving, Sebastian told himself. But he'd had to see her up close. Had to look at her, even though she belonged to some other man now.

There'd been no choice on his part.

He wasn't that strong, hadn't had the time, since arriving yesterday, to reinforce his shield against the only woman he'd ever allowed himself to love. He wanted to look into her eyes just one more time.

Maybe, if he was lucky, there'd be nothing there. For either of them.

"I'm all right." Never really talkative, he knew his reply sounded more stilted than even he could bear. Without thinking, he took her hand, to shake it.

To touch her.

"You look good." His eyes swept over her swollen form and he forced himself to smile. "I think the proper term is *glowing.*"

"That's the heat," she answered dismissively.

Damn you, Sebastian, why did you walk out on me? Why did you leave me, wondering where you were? And why in the name of heaven are you back now?

But he was back and she had to deal with it. Like a soldier, Stephanie squared her shoulders. "Are you back for a visit?"

The slight smile on his lips turned enigmatic. "It's a little more complicated than that," he told her.

God, but you look good, Stevi. Too good.

Sebastian felt old urges rising up, as if they'd never faded away. Maybe they never had.

He had no business feeling that for her now.

He glanced over her head. There was a small, trendy coffee shop with half a dozen tables for two scattered out before it. New, he thought. Everything was new except for the way he felt about her.

Leave it alone. Say goodbye and go, he told himself.

He took a chance, knowing he shouldn't. "Maybe we could step out of the sun somewhere, have a cup of coffee for old times' sake and I—"

There is no "old times' sake," Sebastian, she

wanted to yell at him. Instead, she looked at him with a coolness that belied the churning emotions scrambling through her. With a snap of her wrist, Stephanie pulled her hand free as if it were being scalded.

"I don't think that would be very wise."

Well, what had he expected? Still, disappointment shredded the veneer he was attempting to construct around himself.

"Sure, I understand. Jealous husband, eh?" He had no idea why he'd even said that.

Deep blue eyes, eyes he'd loved to get lost in, cut him dead. "You lost the right to ask questions like that a long time ago, Sebastian."

With that, she turned away, knowing if she didn't, she'd probably do something stupid, like throw her arms around him. Or demand to know why he'd hurt her the way he had. It would have been a humiliating waste of breath for her.

In seven years, Sebastian had never once seen fit to write to her, to call her, to get in contact some way and tell her why he had done what he had. She had no intentions of lowering herself now to ask. There was no reason for it. She knew the reason he'd left. Without her money—because her father would have cut her off without a dime—Sebastian hadn't wanted her and she'd accepted that, accepted it no matter how much it had hurt.

Her head held high, Stephanie walked to her car with as much dignity as she could gather. There was absolutely nothing to be gained by staying and talking to him, she argued with herself. If she remained too long, Sebastian would see that there was a part of her that still, stupidly, cared for him. A part that had never let go, no matter how much she pretended that she had.

Numbly, quietly, he watched her. Watched her get into her car and start it up. As he stared after her, he vaguely noticed the vehicle's color, make and license number like peripheral details of a dream he was trying to shake off.

There was no point to this, Sebastian told himself. He'd just been passing through the small strip mall. There were a couple of videos his mother had requested sitting on the passenger side of the old car he'd driven here all the way from Seattle, Washington. He glanced at them now. If he didn't get going, they were going to melt into the upholstery.

Damn, but seeing her had jarred his heart.

He didn't need things like that. His life had been jarred enough. He had things to see to. He didn't need this trip down a path he hadn't been allowed to take.

Like everything else, he thought, he'd find a way to deal with it. It was just going to take some time, that was all.

Just as he opened the driver's side of his car, Sebastian heard the screech of tires in the distance behind him. Instinct had him swinging around to look back in Stephanie's direction.

He'd turned just in time to see a large black sport

utility vehicle trying to swerve to avoid hitting Stephanie's car.

The maneuver was not successful.

The SUV's blunt nose clipped Stephanie's left front, sending it spinning as metal met metal. The two vehicles groaned from the impact.

She was hurt.

The thought throbbed in his brain.

Hardly aware of shoving his car keys into his pocket, Sebastian grabbed his medical bag and was running toward Stephanie's car before the image of the actual crash had a chance to completely sink in.

Chapter Two

People, drawn by the sound of the crash, were beginning to gather in a large circle around the two vehicles that had wound up crushed nose to nose. Clearly shaken but apparently unhurt, the fortyish driver of the SUV got out, a dazed expression beneath the day-old stubble on his face.

His eyes widened in fear when he saw that there was no movement in the front seat of the other, much smaller car. "I didn't see her," he cried to no one in particular. "I swear I didn't see her pulling out."

A murmur of voices debated the visibility that had been afforded between the two vehicles as Sebastian pushed his way through the crowd, using his medical bag as a shield.

"Let me through," he ordered, fighting a sick feeling as his heart lodged itself in his throat. "I'm a doctor."

Exercising sheer determination, he forced himself not to react to the situation in any other manner except strictly professional. He was afraid to allow his fears free rein. They would only impede what might need to be done.

He didn't like what he saw.

Stephanie's eyes were shut when he yanked open the door on the driver's side, and there was blood mingling with her blond hair from a cut on her forehead. The thought of internal injuries had his gut tightening in cold anticipation.

"Stephanie, can you hear me?" he demanded roughly.

The voice reached out to her across a bridgeless chasm, pulling at her. Drawing her across.

It felt as if each of her eyelids weighed in at ten pounds each as she struggled to open them. She found that it took a concentrated effort to form words. Effort to cut through the pain that was tightening around her like a sharp-toothed vise, stealing her breath away. Stephanie had to push the words out.

"You're shouting," she said hoarsely, each syllable throbbing in her head, making it ache. "Why shouldn't I be able to hear you?"

Relief spread over him in one huge, overwhelming

wave. She was conscious. Maybe the cut on her forehead was the worst of it.

Sebastian squatted down beside her, looking into her pupils. He saw no remarkable dilation. "Do you know what day it is?"

Someone was pounding on her head with an anvil. She touched her hand to the pain and felt something sticky against her fingers.

"Third worst day of my life." She felt Sebastian remove her hand from her forehead. "Maybe the second," she amended.

Concerning himself exclusively with her condition, he didn't allow himself to speculate about what she was referring to. With sure, quick movements, Sebastian examined the cut on her forehead and decided it was minor, then passed his hands over each of her limbs to check for any breaks. There were none.

Stephanie found she had to fight to remain conscious. Her head insisted on sending things swirling around. Vaguely she felt Sebastian's probing hands.

"Hell of a time to get fresh with me, Sebastian," she rasped weakly. "There're witnesses."

His eyes met hers for a moment. She was teasing. For a second, he was propelled across the years, to another time, when teasing had reflected the easy feelings between them.

"Just making sure nothing's broken," he assured her. His hand on hers, he sat back on his heels. "There doesn't seem to be."

It took two beats before her breath returned to her lungs. That had been a particularly bad one.

"Wrong, Sherlock," she managed to say. "I think my water just has."

Damn it, she was going into labor. He could see by the white-knuckled way Stephanie was clutching at his arm. He should have guessed as much. "You're due?"

"Actually," she gasped, bracing herself, afraid of another wave of pain, "I'm two weeks early."

Grabbing onto the steering wheel, Stephanie tried to drag herself out of the car using leverage. To her surprise, she felt Sebastian suddenly taking hold of her arms and easing her out of the vehicle.

Her knees buckled and she would have sunk to the ground if he hadn't been holding her.

This was it, she thought, trying vainly not to panic. Her heart began to hammer erratically.

Ignoring the people around them, ignoring the recent past, she returned to a place in her life when all she had was Sebastian and looked to him for help. She had no other choice.

"Oh, God, Sebastian, I think they're coming."

"They?" His eyes darted toward her belly. Multiple births? He'd thought she'd looked too large to be carrying just one.

She nodded her head and instantly regretted it as fresh pain assaulted her temples. "Twins. I'm having twins."

Great.

He wouldn't allow himself to emotionally dwell on it any longer than that. Looking over his shoulder, Sebastian singled out an older woman who was standing almost directly behind him.

"Call 911," he instructed her. "We need an ambulance."

"We need a lot more than that," Stephanie cried, digging her nails into his bare forearms as she struggled to keep from sinking into the pain again. "They are *really* coming." She couldn't emphasize the word enough.

It was common for first-time mothers to panic, Sebastian thought, and Stephanie had just had an accident to strip away her composure and compound her fear. Still holding her, he did his best to sound reassuring.

"Your contractions must have only started a couple of minutes ago."

She would have laughed at that if she'd had the strength. "A lot you know. They started early this morning."

She'd actually made a mental note to call Dr. Pollack as soon as she picked up the prescription she'd forgotten to get yesterday. She couldn't seem to think clearly these days. Everything had gotten all jumbled ever since she'd received news of the car accident that had taken Holly and Brett out of her life and the lives of the children she was carrying.

Now it looked as if making the call was a moot point. If these contractions racking her body were any indication of what was to come, these babies were going to be born long before Dr. Pollack could manage to get here.

She realized that Sebastian was asking her a question and tried to focus on it.

"What?"

"I said, how far apart are they?" he repeated, raising his voice. "The contractions," he added for good measure. She looked so dazed he wasn't sure if she was following him.

"Why?" She stared at him blankly. "Are you going to boil some water?" The sarcastic question came out of nowhere. In pain, angry, she just wanted to lash out at someone. His sudden reappearance after a seven-year absence and his close proximity made Sebastian the likeliest candidate.

"I'm a doctor," he told her simply, his mind working feverishly as he calculated the chances of his forgetting about waiting for the ambulance and just driving to the nearest hospital with Stephanie himself. "An ob-gyn."

A doctor.

The news stunned her enough to make her forget her pain, at least for a moment. He'd made it. He'd become a doctor. Pride slipped its arms around her, reaching across the bridge of years back from a time when such knowledge would have given her immense pleasure.

Clamping down on her pain, Stephanie looked at him. This is what he'd once told her he wanted to be. Something her father had jeered he would never become. "So, you finally made it."

The words were whispered, and at first he thought he'd imagined them. Raising his eyes, he looked at her. She'd always been the one who had faith in him. She and his mother.

"Yes, I did."

And then she was sinking against him, her energy obviously stolen by the force of the latest contraction. Balancing his medical bag in one hand, Sebastian scooped her up in his arms and looked around. He had to find someplace to make her comfortable.

Turning, he saw the woman he'd instructed to call 911 holding up her small cell phone in the air. "They're coming," she announced.

"Good." With any luck, they wouldn't get here after the fact. But he was beginning to strongly doubt that.

As if reading his expression, a young redhead in tight jeans and an even tighter T-shirt waved to get his attention.

"Here," she called to him. "You can put her down inside my van." Hurrying around to the rear of a light blue van, she unlocked the double doors and threw them open. "The floor covering doubles as a mattress," she said proudly.

As people moved out of his way, Sebastian lost no time in crossing to the van. He managed to place Stephanie on the floor just as she sank all five nails into his arm again. He could almost feel the impact of the contraction right along with her.

"You rip my arm off, I'm not going to be able to use it to help you," he warned, trying to summon a smile for her benefit. The result barely curved his mouth.

Getting into the van beside her, Sebastian crouched on his heels and reached for the doors. Stephanie was going to need privacy. His eyes met the woman's. It was, after all, her van.

"Thanks." He indicated Stephanie beside him. "You want to come inside…?"

But the woman was already backing away, her face growing slightly pale beneath the bold makeup she wore. As if afraid he'd pull her inside, she shoved her hands into her back pockets.

"That's okay, I'll just wait for the paramedics and tell them where you are."

To forestall any further debate, the woman then closed both van doors herself, locking out the curious stares of the people who had not dispersed.

They were alone. Alone in some stranger's van. Alone with the hurtful past and a present that threatened to physically rip her in half. Stephanie wished she could get up and walk out, but that was totally beyond her power at the moment.

Still, she didn't have to make this easy. "What makes you think I'm going to let you help me?" Her breathing began to grow more and more labored.

Same old Stevi, stubborn as hell. He tried to ignore the wave of affection that came out of nowhere.

"I don't think you have much of a choice in the matter, Stevi." With effort, Sebastian drew her up until he had her back flush with the side of the van. It would be better for her this way, since there was no one to prop up her back. "Unless you want to do an imitation of a pioneer woman. In which case, I'll take you over to the nearest wheat field and you can take it from there."

Perspiration was soaking not only her dress, but her scalp as well. Any second, it was going to start dripping into her eyes. She blinked it away. "You do have a black heart, you know that?"

Despite the gravity of the situation, Sebastian looked at her for a long moment.

"Yes," he said quietly, "I know. But that's neither here nor there right now." He looked around the interior of the van. Aside from what looked like a small laundry basket that was holding some canned goods, the van was pretty much empty. He would have preferred far less of a challenge. "You're sure it's twins?"

"I'm sure." She began fisting her hands, bracing herself. "Either twins, or just about the biggest baby on record."

He saw her blanch and grasp for strands of the rug beneath her. "Another contraction?"

She could barely nod, concentrating hard on not letting this latest onslaught of pain tear her in half.

She refused to be one of those screamers people were always ridiculing.

"Maybe you…are…a doctor at that," she panted. The contraction receded, leaving her more exhausted than it found her. Drained, she tried to collect herself sufficiently to prepare for the next one.

She had barely forty seconds.

"Another one?" he asked incredulously. Her contractions were coming faster than he'd anticipated. The fastest birth he'd ever attended was just under three hours. This was beginning to have the makings of just under three minutes.

Stephanie's lips were dry and she felt them cracking as she bit into them. Nobody had warned her it was going to be this awful. But then, no one had told her she was going to be giving birth in a parked oven in the middle of a strip mall parking lot, attended by a man she wasn't supposed to love any longer.

"Sharp," she retorted, vainly trying to grab something to hold on to. But there was nothing to wrap her hands around, nothing to help commute the force of the pain she felt.

Straining to hear the siren of an approaching ambulance he knew wouldn't make it in time, Sebastian threw back the hem of her dress. Unless he missed his guess, the curtain was going up and it was show time.

A quick examination told him he'd guessed correctly. "You're fully dilated."

Oh, boy, this was a big one. Don't scream, don't

scream, she thought frantically. ''Tell…me…something…I don't…know.''

Sebastian looked at her then, just one small, stray look spared in her direction. What would she say if he took her up on that? If he told her something she didn't know? That he, despite all efforts to the contrary, still loved her. Would probably always love her no matter what, to the end of his days. That *he* knew, and it was a cross he knew he had to bear.

But there was no point in sharing that with her. It was just something he was going to have to deal with himself.

''Never could put anything over on you,'' he murmured, looking around for a blanket or something to wrap around the babies, hoping that he'd overlooked one in the initial inspection of the van.

There was nothing.

''Sebastian!'' Stephanie bit back a shriek as she clutched at his upper arm and arched her back, trying desperately to get as far away from the pain as she could. It only followed.

He hated seeing her like this, hated seeing pain etched into her features without being able to take it away.

''It'll be all right, Stevi.'' Tenderness arrived out of nowhere, filling him as he brushed the damp hair away from her eyes. ''I promise.''

''I want…that…in…writing.'' Damn it, this was a lousy way to have a baby. Babies, she corrected herself. Orphaned and in a parking lot without so much as a clean sheet around to wrap them in.

No, they weren't orphaned. They had her. They would always have her, she vowed silently, her mind winking in and out, threatening to take consciousness with it. And she would give them all the love she had stored up in her heart. The love she'd never been allowed to give to anyone.

"Sorry," he told her, "afraid I can't oblige you right now. You're just going to have to take my word for it."

Panting, Stephanie struggled to keep from being steamrollered by the next contraction. Her eyes darted to his. His word. As if she could believe anything he said to her. He'd lied to her once, what was to keep him from lying again?

"Not likely," she breathed, arching again even though she knew it did no good. The pain found her no matter where she moved.

He heard her nails striking the floor's metal border as she again tried to grab on to something to hold. There had to be something he could give her. He thought of his wallet. Pulling it out of his pocket, he wrapped his handkerchief around it.

"Here, bite down on this."

At any other time, she would have questioned his judgment, thinking he was crazy. But this wasn't any other time, this was a unique, dire time and she needed something to help divert the pain, to channel the fearsome energy traveling through her body, however strange that "something" might be.

Grabbing the white linen-wrapped wallet, Stephanie clamped her teeth down on the slightly curved leather just as another contraction scooped her up and tossed her into its midst.

This one was the worst ever.

He heard the muffled scream. Just like Stevi, trying so hard to get through this without a show of pain, he thought. Some things, apparently, never changed. She'd always hated a show of weakness, however justified.

"Soon, Stevi, soon," he promised.

Spitting out the wallet, she panted. "Soon… nothing…I…want this…over with…*now*." Exhaustion threatened to overpower her as she fought to bring life into the world. "What's…taking…so…long?"

Long was a relative word, he thought. To him this was happening almost at lightning speed. "All right, I see a head, Stevi. On the count of three, I want you to push. You hear me?" Glancing up, he saw her nodding her head. "One, two—"

Pulling her shoulders in, Stephanie was pushing before he ever reached the last number, digging her knuckles into the thin floor padding and practically lifting herself off the floor.

"Three," Sebastian said even though it was after the fact. He glanced up to see her face growing red as she held her breath and strained with all her might. "All right, stop."

Like a punctured balloon, Stephanie collapsed against the side of the van, panting not because it was part of the exercise, but because she couldn't draw in enough air into her lungs. It felt as if she'd just run a ten-mile marathon in less than a minute.

"I'm…beginning…to…understand…why…they…call…it…labor."

His mouth curved and he found himself wanting to hold her, to comfort her, but that wasn't his function in this, nor was it his place. There was a husband out there somewhere, a husband who should have, by all rights, been attending this instead of him.

The flash of jealousy was unexpected, uncalled-for and unprofessional. But it was there, nonetheless, red-hot and hard.

Sebastian forced himself to think like a doctor. "You're doing fine, Stevi." They were almost there. "Now I want you to push again. This time," he cautioned, "wait until three."

She sneered at him. She was being torn apart and he was trying to make her obey orders like some kind of tin soldier or lapdog. She'd like to see him get through this insane tug-of-war she was experiencing.

With a new contraction overtaking her before the old one left, Stephanie didn't even wait until the count of two before she began to push again with all her might, this time lifting herself off the floor.

"Stevi—" But it was too late. Sebastian could

only pray she hadn't ruptured something. "I've got the head, Stevi. Now push, push a little more."

She didn't think she could. Squeezing her eyes shut tight, she bore down again, biting back a guttural sound that echoed in her throat, demanding release.

"That a girl, Stevi, the baby's coming."

"I...already...know...that."

She had to push out the shoulders now. The hardest part. He tried to divert her attention from the pain he knew had to be consuming her. "Do you know the babies' sex?"

"Didn't...ask. It was...supposed to be...a surprise."

Holly and Brett had opted not to know, so she hadn't asked to be told, either. Now she deeply regretted that they hadn't found out when they'd had the chance. At least they would have known if they were the parents of boys or girls, or one of each. She ached for their loss. And her own.

Perspiration poured into her eyes, stinging them. Wasn't this ever going to be over?

Out of the haze of pain, she heard Sebastian ordering her, "Push, Stevi, push."

"I *am!*" she shrieked, the cry bursting from her swollen lips.

Smooth as butter, Sebastian thought as the baby all but slid into his hands.

Of course, he doubted that Stephanie felt that way about it, but then she was on the side that was doing all the work. Experiencing a myriad of feelings that only marginally had to do with the customary ones he felt whenever he attended the miracle of birth, Sebastian looked down at this latest citizen of the world.

"Still want it to be kept a surprise?"

"No...damn it." Was he cruel enough to play games when she was so exhausted? "What...is...it? Boy or girl?"

"You have a girl, Stevi."

He heard Stephanie suck in her breath. The second twin was on its way. Unable to hold the newborn, Sebastian took off his shirt and wrapped it around the baby. Quickly dumping out the canned goods, he placed her into the laundry basket.

"All right, let's see if she has a little brother or sister."

"Easy...for...you...to...say," Stephanie managed to reply before the process began again in earnest, even harder this time than before. The pain ripped through her with long, sharp knives. "Oh, God, I'm...going...to...die."

Stephanie heard him draw in his breath, as if bracing himself for a fight. "Not on my shift you're not."

She sincerely hoped Sebastian had learned to keep his word better than he had before.

Chapter Three

Stephanie could have sworn she heard the distant wail of sirens in the background.

Or maybe those were just the noises ricocheting in her head, mixing with the vast array of lights and pain all swirling around within her mind and her body as she strained to give birth to the second twin.

This baby felt larger than the first. Too large to push out. Even her scalp began to tingle as she strained. Sharp needles ran up and down her body, pricking her from the inside out.

She would have never thought she could endure this much pain and still survive.

Sebastian's command of "push" echoed in her brain. Stephanie dug her elbows in close to her side, searching for some small scrap of energy to draw on. There seemed to be none within her reach.

Tense, on his knees in front of Stephanie, Sebastian placed his hand beneath the small head, supporting it as it emerged.

She was almost there, he thought. But there was a mile of pain between "here" and "there."

"That's it, that's it, Stevi, just a little more," he coached, feeling his own breath hitch within his throat. "Just a little more. We're almost there."

"We?" she panted, opening eyes that had been almost screwed shut with the effort she was putting forth. What was he doing without his shirt on? Had he been like that all along? She couldn't remember. "You...want...to...take...over?"   Breathlessness notwithstanding, the question had a sarcastic bite to it.

Sebastian flashed her a grin as a fragment of the past echoed through his mind in response to the arch question she'd thrown at him. There was no daunting her fighting spirit, even now.

"Wouldn't know where to begin, Stevi. You're doing much too good a job yourself."

Before his eyes, Stephanie stiffened, her whole body growing rigid. He recognized the signs. The final thrust was coming whether she was up to it or not. He forced himself to ignore the exhaustion imprinted on her features.

"Now, stop stalling and get those shoulders out, Stevi."

He would have never spoken to any of his patients this way, no matter how well he knew them. But Stephanie always did better when she was goaded, when someone challenged her. It seemed only natural that she'd approach giving birth the same way.

So he goaded her.

He saw the flicker of anger in her eyes. God, but he had missed her. Missed the sound of her laughter, even the sound of her raised voice as she rode headlong into verbal battle with him. She'd never been anything short of magnificent.

Sebastian banked down his thoughts—thoughts that were not his to think about. She was another man's wife now and the past belonged where it was, in the past.

The myriad of feelings flashed through him in a single intake of breath, less time than it took her to bear down for that one last push she had to make. Beside him, the baby's twin was mewling in the basket, a good, healthy sound. And in the background, he thought he heard the ambulance approaching.

Too late, guys, she's almost finished, he thought, relieved that this part of Stephanie's ordeal was almost over.

The muffled, high-pitched noise caught his attention. Sebastian instinctively raised his eyes to her face for a second. Lips parted, teeth clenched together to keep back any sounds and writhing in pain, Stephanie looked as if she was going to turn purple.

"You can scream, you know," he told her. "It actually helps."

But she merely shook her head adamantly from side to side, refusing to be reduced to this most common of common denominators. She wasn't going to allow herself to scream. This wasn't the way it was going to happen. "No" was all she could manage to expel through her lips without running the risk of doing exactly what she was trying not to do.

"There you go, Stevi," he announced, his voice taking on the width and breath of excitement as the infant's shoulders became visible. With one hand beneath the tiny back to support it, Sebastian eased the baby out.

"What...what..." Near collapse, Stephanie didn't have enough strength or breath left within her to form the question.

She didn't have to. Sebastian anticipated it. "You have a boy, Stevi. One of each. You and your husband'll be evenly matched." He had no idea what made him say that, or what to do with the sharp, hot stab of pain in the center of his chest when he made the remark.

With both her head and body throbbing from the effort she'd just put forth, Stephanie hardly heard what he was saying. Except that she had a daughter. And a son. Was she going to be equal to them? Was she going to be able to give them everything they needed, the perfect life they would have had before a blue Chevy, jumping the light, had ended Holly and Brett's lives?

I'll try, she silently vowed to people who were not there and to the two who were. *I promise I'll try.*

Her tongue passed over lips that were parched. "Can...I...?"

Again, Sebastian anticipated the words she was trying to say. "Just give me a second to cut the umbilical cords and you can hold them both if you're up to it. They're a little messy," he warned, knowing it would make no difference to her. Not after what she'd just been through to have them. Despite her father's efforts and her refined background, Stephanie had never been one to hang back just because everything was not pristine. She could always be counted on to charge in no matter what.

He supposed it was one of the first things that had attracted him to Stephanie. Her unpretentious zest for life.

Before Stephanie could summon the energy for a response, the van's rear doors were suddenly being opened. A glaring sheet of sunlight filled the newly created space, framing the figure of a man in a dark blue uniform who peered into the interior of the vehicle.

"Everything all right in here?" he asked, coming inside.

Sebastian reacted the instant the doors were being opened. He threw the hem of Stephanie's dress back down over her legs before turning to look at the person who was climbing in. The paramedics had arrived. It was time to retreat.

"Just in time to take the lady and her kids to the hospital," Sebastian told the older man, moving out of the way.

Even as he did so, he felt a reluctance taking hold. He wanted to remain, to hang around in case she needed him. Which was exactly why he had to get out. With the paramedics on the scene, there was no excuse he could tender that would allow him to stay, other than his own desire.

But desire, dormant or not, had no place here. Stephanie was a wife and a mother and he had nothing to do with either.

The baby he still had in his arms squirmed. Something tightened in his chest. This child could have been his. Stephanie could have been his.

If he hadn't been so damnably noble.

"Sure looks that way," the paramedic was saying. "And you look like you could use a shirt," he commented.

Sebastian looked down. He'd all but forgotten that he'd stripped his shirt off to wrap the first twin in. "I guess I could at that."

"I think we've got something we can fix you up with in the ambulance. You did a great job—" the man glanced at the opened black bag "—Doc. Took us only fifteen minutes to get here from the time we got the call. You are one fast lady," he said, giving

Stephanie a toothy, genial grin. "Lucky for you he came along."

"Lucky," she murmured, trying to make out whether or not Sebastian was even looking her way. The angle of the invasive light made it difficult for her to make out his expression. Maybe it was better that way, now that the crisis was over.

Another paramedic, younger than the first, entered the van. "Here, let me take him," he offered, nodding at the infant in Sebastian's arms.

"There're two," Sebastian told him, indicating the tiny being in the laundry basket.

It occurred to him as he surrendered the baby to the paramedic that he'd delivered and held nearly twenty babies so far in his budding career, yet he was far more aware of giving up this one than he had been of the very first infant he'd delivered.

That little boy should have been his hallmark, not this nameless little creature.

But then, he hadn't loved that first baby's mother as he did this one's. *Once.* Sebastian underlined the word firmly in his mind, knowing he would have no peace otherwise.

What had been was not now. He had to remember that. Seven years had passed. Seven years of sunrises and sunsets, of life moving on.

"There're two in here, Murphy," the second paramedic called out to someone standing outside the van. "Call Bedford General and tell them to get two more bassinets ready."

"Harris Memorial," Stephanie corrected him, relieved that she could gather together enough breath to form more than just a single isolated word at a time. "My doctor's at Harris Memorial."

The older paramedic looked at her apologetically. "Sorry, ma'am, we've got to take you to the closest hospital in the area. I don't have the authority to just arbitrarily pick another—"

Sebastian cut him off. "I'm on staff at Harris Memorial. Whatever paperwork has to be done to get her there, I'll take care of it."

It was a lie, one he figured he could bluff his way through once the time came. Harris Memorial was the hospital where his application was pending as he waited to be accepted. It wasn't a done deal yet. But he didn't want Stephanie subjected to any more undue agitation. In the total scheme of things, he felt he owed it to her.

The older paramedic exchanged looks with his partner, and then he nodded his assent.

"Okay, you're the doc. I'll square it with dispatch later. Guess that means you'll be riding along with the mother in the ambulance." He made the assumption without waiting for a comment.

Sebastian paused, trapped. It hadn't been his intention to accompany Stephanie to the hospital. He was just going to step out of the van and out of her life again, returning home with the videos fate had had him come get just at this exact moment in time.

But after what he'd just said, he didn't see that he had much choice in the matter.

"Guess so," he agreed. He purposely avoided looking at Stephanie. But he could feel her eyes on him.

Emerging out of the van, he stepped into a surprising round of applause.

The people who'd gathered around the initial scene of the accident, including the owner of the black SUV, had obviously all hung around to find out if Stephanie had indeed given birth.

"What did she have?" someone called out.

Sebastian didn't bother trying to attach a face to the voice, merely turned in its direction. "A girl and a boy."

Suddenly, there was a slightly disheveled man in his late thirties at his side, a dog-eared, much-used notepad in his hand.

"Can I get your name?" the man pressed, his pencil poised over a new page. When Sebastian looked at him quizzically, the man added, "I'm from the *Bedford World News,*" citing the small, weekly local paper. "Newborns Make Their Appearance in Apothecary Parking Lot," he declared, using his hands to frame an imaginary headline for an article. He grinned, satisfied. "It's a nice human interest piece, don't you think?"

It was on the tip of Sebastian's tongue to say no. He didn't like sharing his privacy, or having Stephanie's invaded. But she wasn't his to protect, and he reminded himself that he was no longer a private man, either. His medical degree had seen to that. Now he had to be available to the general public. On call at all hours. This included during his private hours.

With a certain amount of resignation, he gave the man his name, saying "the woman" hadn't given him hers. In the strictest sense of the word, it was true, she hadn't.

As the local journalist began peppering him with questions, Sebastian took his arm, pulling him back out of the way as the gurney was lifted into the van. Less than two minutes later, it was back out again, with Stephanie tucked in between the wide belts. On either side of her was a paramedic, each holding a whimpering baby. Each infant was now wrapped in a clean white receiving blanket.

"Time to go, Doc," the lead paramedic called out to him from within the vehicle.

Taking his cue with relief, Sebastian acknowledged the man. "Be right there. Sorry, gotta go," he said to the reporter as he quickly got into the ambulance.

"Hey, wait," the journalist called after Sebastian. "I need details."

"Maybe later" was all Sebastian said just before the doors were closed.

With a sigh, Sebastian turned away from the doors to look at Stephanie. He expected her to say something about the reporter. Instead, he found that she was asleep. The strain of giving birth had finally gotten to her, draining her.

Sebastian sat down gingerly beside her. It was better this way, he thought, resisting the urge to take her hand in his. He'd do what was necessary to get her admitted into the hospital, and once that was taken care of, he'd slip away. He intended to be long gone before Stephanie's husband came on the scene.

He felt his jaw tightening. In his present emotional state, he strongly doubted if he could behave in a civil, detached manner. Not in this case. He didn't believe in putting himself into situations where he wasn't in control, and it didn't take a genius to know that right now, his control was nil.

"Here, Doc, it's the best we've got, I'm afraid." Sebastian looked up to see the first paramedic offering him a blue shirt that resembled his.

Taking it, he put it on. "Thanks."

"I think your shirt's ruined." The paramedic looked at the wadded-up article. "Unless you've got a wife who works miracles."

"No," Sebastian said quietly, looking down at Stephanie. "No wife, no miracles." Seeing her sleeping like that, a thousand thoughts ran pell-mell through his head. He couldn't seem to stop them.

He remembered the last time he had seen her like this…

The *only* time he had seen her like this, Sebastian corrected himself.

The sentimental smile came out of nowhere, unbidden as he relived moments he'd locked away more than seven years ago. He hadn't meant for the things to get out of hand that night, but one thing had led to another and he had made love with her.

Beautiful, exquisite love. Innocent and pure. He could feel his breath evaporating now as he remembered it.

Locked away in his mind or not, that single night was probably what had sustained him through all these long, lonely years.

And what had haunted him.

There was no need for him to remain.

In truth, it turned out that there really was no reason for him to have come in the first place. In true Stephanie fashion, Stephanie had taken care of all the details way ahead of time and registered herself at the hospital against her due date.

He was surprised to discover that Stephanie was preregistered under her maiden name. But then, Stephanie had always been so fiercely independent, retaining her name was something that would have been typical of her, Sebastian realized.

Since the paperwork had been taken care of ahead of time, there was no need for him to fill out any forms. And no need for him to remain any longer.

With no excuse to hide behind, Sebastian made his way to the public phones to call a cab that would take him back to the car he'd left back in the strip mall's parking lot. When he heard the hospital's PA system go off, he didn't really pay attention to it. It had been doing so with a fair amount of regularity since he had arrived with Stephanie. The names being paged only vaguely registered in the peripheral corners of his mind.

This time the name over the PA system did more than just vaguely float through his brain. Sebastian paused to listen. The doctor being paged had the same last name as he had.

"Dr. Caine, please report to the fifth-floor nurses' station."

Had to be a different Dr. Caine, he thought. After all, it wasn't that unusual a last name and no one knew he was here.

"Dr. Sebastian Caine," the voice was saying, "please report to the fifth-floor nurses' station."

So much for it not being him, he thought. But why were they paging him?

Unless—

Worried, afraid that something had suddenly gone wrong with Stephanie, he hurried back to the bank of elevators he'd just left in the rear of the building. Pressing the up button, he waited exactly two beats before considering taking the five flights up via the stairwell.

But as he turned to go toward the stairs, the doors of the elevator car farthest away from him opened. Pivoting on his heel, he did an about-face and hurried into the emptying car.

Impatient, trying not to speculate why he'd suddenly been paged, he punched the button marked five. It felt like an eternity before the elevator reached the fifth floor.

With his lanky stride, it took him less than five seconds to make it from the elevator to the nurses' station.

"I'm Dr. Caine," he told the nurse who was just beginning to leave the area. "I was just paged to come here. Is something wrong with Ms. Yarbour-ough? The woman who was just brought in with twins," he added when the nurse looked at him blankly.

"There's nothing's wrong with Stephanie, Doctor. On the contrary, she couldn't be more right."

Sebastian turned around to see a cool-looking, slender blonde wearing a white lab coat and a warm smile walking toward him, her hand extended in greeting.

"I'm Sheila Pollack, Stephanie's doctor," she told him, shaking his hand. Her sharp eyes quickly took measure of the man before her. She liked what she saw. Cool competence. And there was something in his eyes, something she couldn't quite read but that had the markings of concern. The man had obviously gotten more than just professionally involved. "I just wanted to tell you that you did a fine job."

Relieved, Sebastian mentally upbraided himself for jumping to dark conclusions. But then, in all fair-ness, there hadn't been all that many bright spots in his life to draw on. Stephanie had represented one of the very few. And Stephanie would have been enough, if…

His thoughts weren't supposed to be going in that direction any longer, he chastised himself silently.

Never comfortable with praise, Sebastian acknowledged the woman's compliment with a careless shrug. "She made it easy."

Sheila laughed. The look in her eyes was one of familiarity, even though they hardly knew each other. Between them, they shared Stephanie, and for Sheila, that was enough to make a start. "Stephanie doesn't make anything easy."

He smiled then. "No, I suppose she doesn't." He had to be getting back. He had a feeling the tapes he'd left on the front seat of his car were melting. "Well, Dr. Pollack, if there's nothing else—"

"But there is," Sheila told him, interrupting. "She's asking for you."

Chapter Four

Stupid to feel nervous like this.

Sebastian upbraided himself as he walked down the corridor to Stephanie's room. He'd entered hundreds of hospital rooms. None, not even his first one as a medical student, had ever made his palms feel as if they were damp.

Unconsciously drawing in a deep breath, Sebastian pushed the door open and peered in. Despite the summons, he was hoping that she was asleep. That way, he could say he had stopped by as asked, but would be off the hook.

She was awake.

The hook sank in a little deeper.

"Hi." As he said it, the single-word greeting

sounded particularly lame and hollow to him, given their history and what they'd just gone through together.

She didn't think he'd come, even though she'd asked Sheila to page him for her. She thought that he'd just leave the hospital. Now that he was here, she wasn't sure what to say, or even why she was putting herself through this.

Too late now for second thoughts, she told herself.

Stephanie pressed the remote attached to her bed and the upper portion began to rise, allowing her to look straight at him instead of up.

"Hi."

He nodded over his shoulder toward the corridor beyond the closed door. "Met your doctor. She said you wanted to see me."

The irony of the words struck her. *More than you'd ever know, Sebastian. More than you'd ever even begin to guess.*

Silence played through the room, drawing itself out, encompassing both of them.

There were hundreds of questions crowding her head, and a hundred more accusations and recriminations beyond that. But she knew the futility of rehashing things. Nothing would be settled by bringing up the past and nothing would be resolved. What was done was done. He'd made his choice seven years ago, left her after her father had made it apparent to him, her father had told her, that she and the family money were not a package deal. Her father went to great lengths to make sure she was painfully aware of that. That Sebastian had left her because she would no longer be in his will.

Maybe that was why there was such a schism between her and her father now.

Sebastian was waiting for her to say something. Manners were important in the world she came from. Outward badges of breeding that hid a myriad of blemishes, she thought cynically.

Stephanie said the most logical thing that came to mind.

"I didn't get a chance to say thank you for what you did."

Sebastian shoved his hands into his front pockets. His degree, the long, hard years spent earning it as well as the respect of his peers in the medical profession, all fell mysteriously away. For a second, he was just Sebastian Caine again, a seventeen-year-old senior from the wrong side of the tracks, way out of his league by trying to strike up a conversation with the daughter of one of the most well-known lawyers in the state. Never mind that she was his friend's sister. His mouth had turned to cotton just looking at her.

A little like now, he thought.

All he'd had then to see him through was his bravado. That, and an attraction so strong, he couldn't even breathe when he was in the same vicinity as Stephanie.

Sebastian dug deeper now, telling himself he was

a fool for the momentary jolt of insecurity. He'd come a very long way since then. He'd made something of his life, not wasted it away in the pursuit of some meaningless job the way her father had predicted.

In an odd sort of way, he supposed he had her father to thank for all that, for becoming the doctor he was now. It was the image of Carlton Yarbourough's smirking face that had goaded him into meeting challenge after challenge long after he had ceased to willingly go out tilting at windmills. It had been his determination to show the snide bastard up that had made him endure the spirit-draining schedule of holding down two jobs and attending medical school, all on next to no sleep.

Funny how things turned out sometimes. The man who had clearly hated him had become one of the reasons he had attained his goals.

The westerly oriented room embraced the sunlight that spilled into it. Sebastian took another step into the room. Another step closer to her.

"I'm a doctor. If I stumble across a woman giving birth, it's my job to stop and help her. It's clearly spelled out in the Hippocratic oath," he added.

She couldn't help the smile that came to her lips. "Same eloquent way of saying things, I see."

He shrugged carelessly, looking away. The woman had just given birth and wasn't supposed to look enticing in any manner, shape or form. So why did she?

"Yeah, well, can't expect much from a guy dragged up on the wrong side of the tracks, now can you?"

She looked at him, trying to still the numbing pain his cold tone had suddenly generated within her. He'd always been a brooding soul, but not like this. When had he become so bitter?

"I always did," she told him quietly. And she had. Expected great things of him. Which was why having him abandon her without a word of explanation had been so devastating to her.

He laughed shortly. She lied well, he thought. In the end, if they had stayed together, it would have been just like her father said, her soul squashed by a life of deprivation. "Well, that would have placed you in the minority."

She was trying very hard not to let her emotions into this. "I don't think so."

Sebastian looked at her and felt that old feeling wash over him. The one that reduced him in stature and strength. He wasn't going to stay and get pulled in by those huge blue eyes of hers. Wasn't going to stand here, looking at her mouth form words and wishing he could silence it with his own.

He'd only be making himself crazy.

Slowly, he began backing away toward the door. "Look, I've got to be going." He thought of the initial errand that had caused their paths to cross. "There're videotapes dissolving in my front seat." His hand was on the door. "Glad you're okay."

He left before she had a chance to say she was sorry to see that she couldn't say the same for him.

When had he returned to Bedford? How long had he been walking the streets, driving the roads, without letting her know he was here?

Loneliness blanketed her.

Suddenly feeling very, very tired, Stephanie closed her eyes and sank back into her pillow as she slowly lowered the bed down again.

"Did they move the video place to Seattle?" Geraldine Caine's teasing voice reached Sebastian just as he let himself into the house.

Pocketing his key, he turned toward the family room and watched her approaching. Something sad and angry twisted inside of him as he saw her leaning so heavily on the cane that never seemed to leave her side now. He couldn't help remembering the way this bright, vibrant woman had initially encouraged his love of track and field sports by jogging alongside him when he was just a boy.

Now all that seemed left of that woman was her wide smile and that brilliant sparkle in her eyes. Except that right now she looked worried. That was his fault, he thought with a prick of guilt. He knew she was trying not to show just how concerned she must have grown. Being a good mother in her book meant sublimating her own needs, her own fears and putting his life first. It was the way she had always operated. He'd always come first. She'd never said a word when he left home seven years ago. Only that she would always be there for him if he should need her. She was one in a million. Which was why he'd returned when she'd needed him.

"Sorry," he said, tucking the two videos he'd brought in under his arm, "I should have called."

Geraldine had long since come to the conclusion that mothers only stopped worrying once they were dead.

"You're a thirty-year-old man, Sebastian. There's no need to keep your mother apprised of your every move." And then she smiled, creating a small space between the thumb and forefinger she held up. "Maybe a little phone call," she allowed.

She led the way to the kitchen, knowing he had to want a cup of coffee. He'd developed a fondness for the brew at the age of eleven, when he used to come to the restaurant after school and do his homework, waiting for her to get off work. Over the years, his affinity for the drink had only intensified.

Unable to contain her growing curiosity any longer, she turned from the coffeemaker on the counter and asked, "So, what was it that kept you from promptly returning from the video store? An old friend you ran into? A wave of nostalgia that took you past the university?" Filling the two cups that stood waiting on their saucers, she waited for Sebastian to jump in.

He sat down on the stool beside the counter and

pulled the cup and saucer over to him. "The former."

"Oh?" Geraldine laced her own coffee liberally with a creamer, wondering if she was as bad at sounding innocent as she thought. "Who?" Sebastian raised his eyes to hers and then she knew. Knew without his having to say a word. Geraldine felt her mother's heart constrict just a little within her breast. "How is she?"

Sebastian took a long, silent sip, then laughed softly, shaking his head in disbelief. Not that she hadn't managed to do this "magic trick" of hers before. "You know, you really should have never let that mind-reading talent of yours go to waste."

Eyes the same color as his crinkled as she smiled at him, this serious boy who had grown into such a serious man. "Only works on you, I'm afraid. Not much of a calling for mothers to make revelations about their children on the open market."

He thought of the tabloid headline he'd seen recently at the supermarket: Country Star's Mama Sings the Blues About Her Son. "Unless you're the mother of a celebrity," he told her.

Geraldine set down her cup again. "Oh, but I am." She tucked one arm around his and gave him a quick hug. "I'm the mother of an up-and-coming doctor who gave up his budding practice to rush to the side of his ailing, pain-in-the-butt mother."

Leaning over, he kissed the top of her head. Affection laced through him. "You were never a pain in the butt." And then he grinned down at her. "It was more like a pain in the neck."

Relieved that he could still joke after seeing Stephanie, Geraldine feigned a serious expression. "Show a little respect, you hear?"

He drained the coffee cup, then helped himself to another serving. "You started it, remember?"

She watched him set the coffeepot back on the burner. He was agitated. He always drank a lot of coffee when he was agitated, which only made him more so. It was a vicious cycle.

"I'm your mother, I can start anything I want." She sobered, dropping the bantering tone. Treading lightly on the sensitive ground, she approached it again. "So, you didn't answer me. How was she?"

Just as damn beautiful as ever. More. I wish I'd never seen her.

"About to give birth," he replied offhandedly. Though it was hard to maintain his vague tone when he added, "As a matter of fact, I delivered her twins."

Geraldine sank down on the stool, bracing herself against the counter. Her cane clattered to the floor. "She's pregnant?"

Sebastian bent down and retrieved the cane, leaning it against the underside of the counter beside his mother. She nodded her silent thanks.

"Not anymore. Two healthy babies, a girl and a boy, thanks to yours truly. Delivered in the video rental parking lot.'' He added the coda as if he were delivering Shakespearean lines.

Geraldine frowned, having a difficult time assimilating all this. "Right out in the lot?"

It might have come to that. Stephanie had seemed ready to pop. "In a van, actually. Some woman lent it to us when it didn't look as if the ambulance would make it in time. I didn't get her name," he added, realizing only now as he said it. "She probably regretted her random act of kindness the minute she got a load of the inside of her van."

Geraldine shook her head. He'd delivered a baby in the time she'd been watching the clock and twisting her medal almost off its link. "I let you out of my sight for what starts out to be just a few minutes and you run off, playing Dr. Kildare."

He looked at his mother blankly. "Dr. who?"

She waved a hand at him, picking up her cup again. "Never mind, before your time." Taking a long sip, she allowed herself a second to speculate on the situation. "I wonder how her father took all this."

Stephanie's father was the last person he'd concerned himself with. "I couldn't care less." Curiosity arose suddenly, out of nowhere, getting the better of him. "Why should he take this badly? Didn't he approve of her husband?"

Not that he thought Carlton Yarbourough would ever feel that anyone would ever be good enough for his daughter or his son, for that matter. He wondered if Matthew had ever married.

Finishing her coffee, she debated a second cup, then decided against it. "He probably wouldn't have, if there had been one."

Sebastian stared at his mother once the words sank in. "Are you saying she's not married?"

Ruffling his hair, she smiled fondly at him. "Still smart as a whip."

Sebastian ran his hand through his hair, smoothing it back down again. He hadn't seen a ring on Stephanie's hand this morning, but he'd just assumed that her fingers had gotten too swollen to allow her to wear one. It happened often enough in the latter stages of pregnancy.

"How would you know she's not married?" he asked his mother.

Moving the cup and saucer aside, she drew the dish with freshly baked crumb cake on it closer and broke a piece from the side. "What, you didn't think I'd keep track of the woman who broke my son's heart?" Specks of powdered sugar rained down on her lap as she nibbled. "The woman he left town over?"

He looked at her sharply. "I didn't leave town over Stephanie."

When would he admit the truth to himself? "You were accepted by the University of Bedford, one of the best medical schools in the west. You had a scholarship and were all set to attend and then you suddenly turned your back on everything and went clear up the coast to practically Canada. I call that leaving.''

He shrugged, setting his empty cup down. ''I figured it was time.''

She touched his cheek, wishing there was a way to break through the barrier of years and make them fade away, at least for a little while. She would have given anything to return to the years when she could gather him on her lap and be able to soothe away whatever it was that was troubling him.

''No, you didn't, you were getting away.'' And then she smiled.

Confused by her expression, he raised his brow. ''What?''

Taking out a knife, she cut a slice of the crumb cake she'd baked to get her mind off that time and pushed the piece toward him.

''I just had a mental image of trying to gather you on my lap, like I used to.'' Her mouth quirked. ''Funny, I used to hope you and Stephanie would give me a grandson, so I could shamelessly indulge my maternal longings for a few more years, and now Stephanie's given birth....'' She sighed, knowing that she shouldn't be mentioning the woman at all. ''I guess things never go the way you expect them to.''

''No,'' he agreed, ''they don't.''

Time to change the topic. She glanced down at the

two videos he'd placed on the counter. "So, which will it be? *Tango in the Rain* or *Last Man Out?*"

Momentarily lost in thought, Sebastian seemed not to hear her. And then he pushed the second video toward her on the counter. "I think the latter is appropriate, don't you?"

Her hand covering the tape, she raised her eyes to his. She wasn't about to sit by and let him ride roughshod over himself. "Since when did you ever count yourself out?"

He knew his mother well enough to know it wasn't a question. It was a challenge.

There was an entire host of things he knew he should be doing, Sebastian thought the next day.

Making out a list of possible physicians to interview, for one. He needed to attach himself to a medical corporation or at least a prominent medical office, and soon, if he hoped to be accepted by Harris Memorial. It wasn't just a matter of money, or the med-school loan he was still repaying. In town for a little more than two weeks, Sebastian wanted to get back into the thick of things and get busy. He didn't do idle well, never had. Now that his mother was home from the hospital and insisting on doing things for herself, he was at loose ends. He'd hustled and worked most of his life, beginning with a paper route at seven and doing odd jobs for the neighbors in order to bring a little money into the house.

Even though the amount had been small, it eased

his conscience a little, when he saw how hard his mother worked, to be able to give her the meager money he earned. Whatever material things he wanted in his life, he'd always gone out and earned them for himself. It was enough that his mother provided the basic essentials, the most important of which was a loving home life. Without that, the rest, no matter how good it might have gotten, would have been totally meaningless.

He supposed that was one of the things that had attracted him to Stephanie in the first place. In monetary terms, where he had little, she had a great deal. But her home life was far less happy than his. Essentially abandoned by her mother at a young age when her parents were divorced, she lived with a father who ignored her and an older brother who cared about her but was usually too busy to spend any time with her.

He'd been friends with Matthew first, but it was Stephanie who'd roped his heart almost from the first second he saw her. Because she'd grown to mean so much to him in such a short amount of time, he'd taken to bringing Stephanie over to his house. He'd secretly taken pleasure in watching his mother fuss over her and in watching Stephanie respond to the attention and warmth his mother gave her like rain nourishing a thirsty flower.

Somewhere in his naive mind, he'd thought that things would only continue to get better.

Damn it, it wasn't going to get him anywhere, going over all this old ground. All he was doing was just torturing himself.

So why was he driving over to the hospital to see her? What sense did that make? Was he that anxious to rake himself over red-hot coals that should have been allowed to die out a long time ago?

He didn't turn back.

Sebastian drove into the hospital parking lot, finding a place toward the rear. The lot was almost full.

He got out before he was tempted to turn around and go home again. In all likelihood, he would run into her father. Whether to see his grandchildren or take Stephanie to task for bringing shame to the family reputation, the man would probably be there in the room with her when he walked in, Sebastian thought.

Rather than turn on his heel and leave, Sebastian felt himself girding up for the confrontation.

Maybe it would do him good to clear the air after all these years. It would probably twist the old man's gut to know that he was inadvertently responsible for any success Sebastian had achieved, especially since Yarbourough hadn't thought him remotely worthy of his daughter.

Sebastian tried to concentrate on that and not on the way he'd feel, seeing Stephanie again.

Like a man resigned to his fate, he sighed as he walked to the rear of the building and its bank of elevators.

For such a full parking lot, the corridors seemed

remarkably empty. Everyone was probably in the rooms, visiting, he decided, jabbing the up button. The appropriate light went on.

"Dr. Caine?"

He turned around just in time to see Sheila Pollack walking toward him, her hands buried deep in her pockets, a warm smile of greeting on her face.

"I thought that might be you. Checking in on our patient?"

Sebastian wondered if the woman thought he was butting in. Doctors were not unknown to be territorial when it came to their patients. But he saw nothing in her expression to indicate that she wanted him elsewhere.

"No, actually she's...someone I used to know." It sounded so detached, so austere. But there was no place for the words he might have said, had things turned out differently.

Was it his imagination, or was the look in the woman's eyes one of sympathy and understanding? Stephanie wasn't the type to talk about her personal life, so he doubted that the doctor knew anything about him. Yet he wasn't mistaken about the look.

"Right, Stephanie said you grew up around here. What brings you back?" she asked. "Are you visiting?"

"Staying," he corrected her. "I've moved back to Bedford."

Sheila looked at him for a second, saying nothing as she quickly arranged her thoughts. The elevator bell sounded, announcing a car's arrival. She placed her hand on his wrist to keep him from taking it. "Do you have a minute?"

He glanced at the car, then decided to let it go. If Yarbourough was there with Stephanie, he was in no hurry to get there. "What's on your mind?"

"Every so often, I let myself go with an impulse." It had been an impulse that had her walking down the beach at twilight with the handsome stranger who would, nine months later, insist on becoming her husband just as their love child was making her way into the world. Impulse, she'd discovered since then, was a very good thing.

"I'm not sure I understand."

Sheila laughed, realizing she'd jumped into the middle again. "My husband says I let my brain get ahead of my tongue and confuse people." She sized him up one last time and then went full steam ahead. "Tell me, Dr. Caine, are you looking to join a medical office?"

Chapter Five

Sebastian paused, wondering if he'd misheard the woman. Just off the laboratory there was a commotion going on near the bank of elevators, and it was possible that his thoughts had somehow gotten incorporated in what he thought he heard Dr. Pollack saying to him.

"Excuse me?"

Ideas she was enthusiastic about had a tendency to rush out of her mouth, tangled up in their own words. Sheila tried to organize them so that the man before her could follow her thoughts.

"I don't know if it's something in the air or the advent of a new century, but whatever it is, I have never been busier," she confided to him. "It seems like every time I turn around, one of my patients is giving birth, and if I want to be someone whom my children actually recognize from something other than a photograph, I'm going to need help. It's either that or start turning new patients away, and I really don't want to do that.'' Especially since almost all of her new patients were referred to her by her existing patients. The word *no* was not readily in her vocabulary.

''So—'' Sheila moved out of the way as another car arrived and the passengers began disembarking ''—if you're planning on settling down in Bedford, I'd be happy to talk to you at length about the possibility of taking you on as a partner.''

She couldn't tell by his expression whether or not she'd struck a viable chord, or if he was searching for a polite way to turn her down. Feeling in her pockets, Sheila searched for a card to give him.

''I know I have a business card in here somewhere.'' Finally locating it in her side pocket, Sheila pulled it out. ''It's a little worn around the edges,'' she apologized, offering it to him. ''But at least the phone number's visible. My office is in the building just across the street. Give me a call when you're ready and we'll talk.''

The public-address system went off and her name was among the three doctors currently being paged. She looked up at the disembodied voice. ''Looks like they're playing my song.'' She flashed him another warm smile. ''See what I mean?''

Touching his arm fleetingly by way of saying goodbye, Sheila was off to answer her page. In a moment, her trim, white-clad figure disappeared around the corner.

It took him a moment to remember to press for the elevator again. Doing so, Sebastian looked down at the pale ivory card in his hand. Dr. Pollack was right, it was worn around the edges, as if she'd been unconsciously playing with it while it was in her pocket. For a second, he studied the embossed script.

He wondered if this was some sort of omen meant to get his attention.

Like running into Stephanie.

He stepped through the parting doors and pressed for the fifth floor. Even though he'd returned home, other than taking care of his mother, he'd been undecided about his course of action. Should he take his mother back with him and set her up in Seattle? Should he move back here and find a position for himself? Admittedly, the latter would probably be easier, at least for his mother.

He wasn't so sure if it would be for him, but one thing was for certain. It felt as if the scales were definitely being tipped toward his remaining in Bedford.

Pocketing the card, he told himself to think about it later. When his head was clearer.

As his knuckles made contact with the door, he heard muffled voices coming from the other side.

Thoughts of a confrontation with Yarbourough returned.

For a second, he debated retreating, leaving the flowers he'd thought to pick up on his way here at the nurses' station. There was no need to give them to Stephanie in person. Besides, the last thing he wanted was to voluntarily encounter Yarbourough.

So what if he's here? You going to turn tail and run? an inner voice mocked.

He wasn't here to see Carlton Yarbourough, he was here to see Stephanie. And to maybe satisfy his curiosity as to what sort of man had turned her head so completely that she'd borne his child—children, he amended—without bothering to marry him. Though she'd tried very hard to perpetrate the role of a wild child to irritate her father, there were some things Stephanie wouldn't do, and having a baby before she was married was one of them—or at least, so he'd thought.

Had she changed that much? And how much of that change was his responsibility?

And then it hit him. In all likelihood, the man belonging to the other voice wasn't her father but the father of her babies.

He'd find another time to intrude. Dropping his hand from the door, Sebastian began to turn away.

His retreat was aborted when he heard Stephanie call, "Come in." There was something in her voice that compelled him to override his common sense. Pushing the door, he walked in.

It wasn't her father or some stranger he didn't know, hovering over her and holding her hand. Instead, standing next to her bed like a martinet sent to do sentry duty, was Matthew, her older brother.

The man who had once been his best friend—until he'd run out on Matthew's sister.

The awkwardness within the small, confining room could be cut with a knife as the three inhabitants looked at one another.

"Matt," Sebastian acknowledged, nodding at him stiffly. Words milled around in his mind like last-minute holiday shoppers in a mall. Not a single one managed to materialize. There was so much to be said, that he said nothing.

"Sebastian." Formal, Matthew's tone echoed his own as he nodded at him.

"And I'm Stephanie," Stephanie announced in a syrupy, singsong voice intended for preschool television viewers of children's shows. She clapped her hands together. Both men looked at her. "Now that we all know one another, boys and girls, let's have some fun."

Sebastian laughed shortly, the jibe breaking through the frost in the room. This was stupid. They'd known each other for years. Or had. And once upon a time, they'd shared secrets and dreams.

"Look, if I'm intruding..." He took a tentative step back toward the door.

Matthew looked to Stephanie for his cue. He was willing to remain if she needed him despite the one o'clock appointment who would be waiting for him in his office.

Good old Matthew, he was almost transparent, Stephanie thought, reading her brother's mind. She squeezed the hand he rested on her shoulder. It hadn't happened until he'd hit his twenties, but he'd finally become the big brother she'd always wanted. Except that now she could fight her own battles.

"It's okay, Matt."

"As long as you're sure." Leaning over, he kissed her forehead. "I'll see you later. Maybe I can convince Father—"

Stephanie could feel her muscles tightening in her jaw. "Don't bother. He obviously doesn't want to come here."

The years at home, more than his career as a corporate attorney, had taught Matthew the virtues of being a peacemaker. "He's just stubborn, Stef, you know that."

In response, she smiled up at her brother. "See you later, Matt," she said, purposely ignoring his last comment.

Passing him on the way out, Matthew nodded at Sebastian, his expression reserved and stoic, as if they hadn't shared so much in years that had gone by. "Sebastian."

The door closed again. Sebastian crossed to Stephanie's bed, glancing over his shoulder. "Is it me, or did the temperature in here just drop by some thirty degrees?"

For a moment, his voice sounded exactly as it had when they were younger and used to talk for hours. But she wasn't going to allow herself to be deceived by some false sense of yesteryear. She had to remain on her guard. No one was ever going to be allowed to hurt her the way he had.

"You can't exactly blame him. The way he sees it, you ran out on both of us. Him and me." She smoothed out the edge of the blanket slowly. "And Matthew was always very protective of me."

The words dragged like raw nettles along the tender underbelly of Sebastian's conscience. He'd cut his ties completely when he'd left, staying in touch only with his mother. She'd come out to visit him several times, but he'd always found excuses not to return to Bedford. After a while, his mother had ceased asking.

He'd missed Matthew's friendship. Almost as much as he'd missed having Stephanie in his life.

"Nice to have someone looking out for you," he commented.

"Yes." *But if I'd had a choice, I would have wanted it to be you.* She nodded at the bouquet in his hand. "So, did you bring those as a visual prop, or do you intend on giving them to me sometime before you leave?" she finally asked when he made no move to do anything but hold the flowers in his hand.

Sebastian looked at her blankly, then down at his hand. Embarrassed, he flushed slightly. He'd forgotten he had them. Feeling like a fool, he thrust the carnations at her. "I thought you might like some flowers. I didn't know if I was overstepping my bounds."

Bringing them up to her face, Stephanie inhaled deeply. The last time she'd been given flowers, they were tiny wildflowers, mixed with dandelions. And he had picked them for her. She blocked the tender feelings threatening to take over.

"I think there's a vase under the sink," she prompted, pointing toward it. "I saw it when they took out the towels."

Clutching the flowers, she watched his back as he turned away, remembering how it felt to run her hands along it, how strong he'd felt to her touch. Back then, she'd thought that nothing could hurt her as long as she was with him. She hadn't realized that he'd be the one to inflict the wound.

She forced herself to look at the bouquet instead. "What do you mean, overstepping your bounds?"

He found the vase and filled it with water. "Maybe your significant other wouldn't like you accepting flowers from an old friend."

The term was almost sterile. And deceptive. "Is that what you are, an old friend?"

Vase in hand, Sebastian turned to look at her. "Yes, I am."

It was on the tip of her tongue to demand to know how he could call himself a friend after the way he'd slashed her heart to pieces by disappearing without a word. Disappearing when she was on the verge of running off with him to any place he named.

But asking would make him see just how deep her wound had gone and she didn't want to let him know that. Knowing would give him power over her and no one was ever going to have that kind of power over her again.

Instead, she shrugged carelessly. "If you say so," she murmured.

He took the flowers from her, their fingers brushing against one another. For a second, his eyes held hers and then he looked away, afraid she would see too much. Afraid he would give things away when it wasn't his place.

"I say so." He set the vase down on the shelf that ran along the wall next to her bed. Stepping back, he pretended to study the flowers. It was a great deal safer than looking at her. The pale blue nightgown she had on definitely wasn't regulation hospital issue and was stirring his imagination something fierce. "You sure this won't cause any problems?"

She had no idea what he was talking about. "With who?"

"Your significant other," he repeated, disliking the term even more the second time than he had the first. Disliking the fact that he had no say in her life anymore.

"You keep saying that, but there is no significant other."

He studied her, wondering how much she'd

changed in the last seven years. He knew he'd changed, grown less angry, more tolerant. But some things remained constant. Like the way he felt about her. "Then it was casual?"

Her patience felt like a wet tissue, about to dissolve. "Was *what* casual?"

Frustration took a second pass at him. He shoved his hands deep into his pockets, his left coming in contact with Sheila's card. He folded it automatically. He had no business even asking her about her private life, no business feeling like this about a woman he'd forced himself to give up so long ago.

But he still heard himself saying, "The union, or whatever you want to call it, that led up to what happened in that woman's van yesterday. You got pregnant, Stevi, and as far as I know, there's been only one immaculate conception on record."

Was that jealousy she saw in his eyes? Sebastian was struggling to maintain his composure, but she knew him too well to be fooled.

But how could he be jealous of her if he'd walked out on her? Was it just some residual possessiveness that was making him behave as if he cared who she slept with?

Stephanie drew herself up, squaring her shoulders. "Yes, but there've been a great many in vitro fertilizations since then."

"In vitro—" He stared at her as his voice trailed away. It didn't make sense. She was too young to worry about her biological clock ticking the years away, too young to opt to be a single mother rather than not a mother at all. She had a great deal of time left before that would become a concern. "Why would you do that?"

"You don't have the right to ask me questions like that anymore." She had every intention of just leaving the words at that, but something within her refused to listen. Something that had once loved him with all her heart. Besides, he did have a right to know about Holly and Brett. He'd been their friend, too, at one time. "They're not my babies, they belong to Holly and Brett."

"Holly and Brett?" She had to mean Holly Duncan and Brett Collier. He thought he remembered his mother mentioning that they had gotten married. "What do they have to do with it?"

Because it was all still so raw, Stephanie gave him the short version. Even so, she could feel tears threatening to gather. "Holly and Brett couldn't have children, so I volunteered."

He stared at her. "You're a surrogate mother?" Stephanie would have been the very last person in the world he would have thought of in that context.

He said it as if she'd just told him that she was really the queen of Venus. "You sound surprised. Didn't you think I had it in me?"

"It's not that...." He stumbled through his words. "It's just that I guess I'm having trouble visualizing you doing something so—"

"Selfless?" she supplied. Maybe she had been a

little spoiled when he'd been part of her life. But that had more to do with getting back at her father than anything else. "People change." She looked at him significantly. "Sometimes they change a great deal."

He'd give her that. He had that coming. And anything else she wanted to lay at his doorstep, he thought.

"So where are they? Holly and Brett," he clarified. "I would have thought they'd be here the second they found out you gave birth." He remembered the couple, as full of life as he had once been full of darkness. "Why aren't they here?"

"Because they can't be anywhere."

He looked at her, confused, and saw the tears suddenly shimmering in her eyes. She swept them away with the back of her hand. A deadness inexplicably filled him.

"Holly and Brett died three weeks ago in an automobile accident. Brett died at the scene, Holly hung on a little while, long enough for me to get to the hospital." She pressed her lips together, trying very hard not to relive the scene. "She made me swear to take care of the babies."

Please, Stef, swear you won't let Brett's mother raise them. Promise me you'll be their mother.

And she had given her word to a dying friend. Stephanie felt her throat closing over.

Sebastian's voice reached out to her over the chasm of the recent past. "Holly and Brett are dead?"

"That's what I said." Dragging her hand through her hair, she took a deep breath. "Sorry, I didn't mean to snap like that. I guess my nerves are a little tender." She forced a smile to her lips that fell short of her eyes by a wide margin. "It's not every day you give birth in the back of some strange woman's van with your ex-lover in attendance. I'm still having a little trouble getting over that." She looked away, trying her best to pull herself together.

He squelched the urge to take her into his arms and hold her. Even if there was no one else in her life, it wasn't his place anymore to comfort her. To hold her.

But the feeling refused to leave.

Sebastian went to look out the window and pretended to be interested in the sailboats he saw bobbing in the harbor.

"So what are you going to do?"

He verbalized the question she'd been asking herself, one way or another, since the accident. Matthew had pushed for her to give the babies up for adoption. But even so, she'd always known, deep down, what course she was going to take.

"What I promised Holly I'd do. Take care of the babies. Raise them as my own, making sure they know how much they were wanted."

It took all he could do not to wince for her. Sebastian knew she was referring to the fact that she had never received that kind of unconditional love from her own parents. Or much of any sort of love

in reality. Her mother had been Carlton Yarbourough's second wife, far more interested in her charity
work, her clubs and her image than she was in the
daughter she'd given birth to. Stephanie had been
unplanned and, for the most part, unwanted by her
father because she had turned out not to be another
son. If not for Matthew, who was really her half
brother, she would have never known any sort of
affection within the cold house she'd grown up in.

He thought of what his own mother had endured.
Granted, times were different and an unwed mother
no longer endured censure the way his had, but there
was still a stigma attached to it.

"You're sure you want to raise them on your
own?" Sebastian ignored the flash of temper he saw
in her eyes. "Even in this day and age, it's still hard
to raise a baby all by yourself, never mind two."

There had never been any question in her mind
whether or not she was equal to the situation. She
was surprised he of all people would ask. "Women
have been doing it since time began."

He turned around to look at her. "Yes, I suppose
you're right." There was a trace of bitterness in his
voice as he thought of his mother again. "I mean,
it's not as if you were some woman from the wrong
side of the tracks."

The flash of anger turned into a regular firestorm.
"If you're delicately referring to the fact that my
brilliant attorney father is now in a position where
he has more money than God, that has no bearing

on my life. In case you missed that little interaction with Matthew earlier, my father and I aren't exactly on the best of terms." Her nightgown slid off her shoulder and she yanked it back, nearly tearing the fabric. "Or any terms, actually, for that matter.

"Despite the fact that my life didn't arrange itself the way I thought it was going to—" she looked at him significantly "—I finally found enough strength to tell my father exactly what I thought of him. I moved out of the family lair quite some time ago." And then a wry smile twisted her lips. "I suppose it didn't hurt to have that money from my grandmother to help see me through while I looked around to 'find' myself."

He knew that it was hopelessly clichéd, but he found himself thinking that she looked magnificent when she was angry. "And did you find yourself?"

"Yes, I did," she told him proudly. "And as it happens, I didn't wander all that far away in the first place. I made something of myself. I have my own web design business and I am good at it. It just took me a little while to pull all the pieces together." Pieces, she added silently, that he had left in his wake. Pieces that had broken apart, too, when she'd lost his baby.

Damn it, why are you here? And why do I have such trouble hanging on to my anger? Why do I want you to hold me even when I want to scratch your eyes out?

"So tell me," she said, doing her best to sound

politely disinterested, "just what is it that you're do-ing here?"

He thought she meant in the hospital. "Unoffi-cially, you're my patient. I thought I'd check and see how you were doing. You're also my friend," he couldn't help adding.

And if she believed that, she deserved everything that had happened to her, she thought. "You're ban-dying that word around and you haven't even a clue as to its meaning."

She was wrong there, but he wasn't about to argue with her. "I'd like to change the status on that."

"Would you?"

He heard the cynicism in her voice. It wasn't something he was accustomed to hearing from her. Despite the raw deal she'd gotten from her parents, despite the poor little rich girl background she had, Stephanie had always been the soul of optimism, a little cocky at times, but always optimistic. He knew that he was at least partially responsible for the change that had come over her.

It wasn't something he was proud of, but some-thing, he knew, that had been necessary.

It was the only time he and her father had agreed, though he would have never told the old man that. Sebastian knew that ultimately, he wasn't any good for her, that he would have only managed to drag her down. The only way he could make himself leave her was by breaking it off cold turkey.

So he had.

"Yes," he told her quietly, reaching for her hand. "I would."

She pulled her hand away as if he'd burned it. "So, exactly what does this 'change of status' mean?"

He let his hand drop to his side. Small steps, he counseled himself. The journey was made with small steps. "It means that when we see each other, neither one of us turns away."

Stephanie blew out a long breath. Easier said than done. "You're going to have to give me some time for that."

He had to be going, Sebastian thought. He'd already stayed longer than he thought he would. "Take all the time you want, I'm not going anywhere. I'm staying in Bedford."

"For how long?"

"Indefinitely."

Stephanie told her heart it had no business leaping up. It didn't listen.

Chapter Six

Well, he'd done it, Sebastian thought, walking down the long, newly remodeled corridors the next day. He'd committed himself for the long haul.

With his mother's health in an unpredictable state, there was really nothing else he could do. Myasthenia gravis with its merciless, random, ever progressive attacks on the muscles of its victims, making them ever weaker, was a nasty enough disease to deal with without his mother having to suffer through being uprooted and transplanted after spending thirty-five years in one place. She was in remission at the moment, but he just couldn't do that to her, not for his own convenience. His mother's friends were here. More important, Geraldine Caine had built up a life here, forged out of tireless hard work and extreme dedication against odds that would have squelched the soul of a lesser person.

Starting out as a waitress, his mother had worked long hours and saved judiciously until the day arrived when she finally bought the restaurant where she had started out at years earlier. And despite all the effort she'd had to put into it, despite all those hours she worked, she always made sure that he never wanted for her presence, her care. There were times he was certain she never slept, that she just lived on batteries.

She'd built the place and its reputation up until now people came from miles around to sample the cuisine instead of just stopping by because the restaurant happened to be there when hunger struck. To take her away from her business would be to kill her spirit by inches. There was no way he could do that.

But he could restrict her and, conspiring with her specialist, he did. She had to cut her hours down. Reluctantly, she'd agreed. But she had good people working for her, so delegating had turned out to be less difficult than anticipated. She just had trouble, he thought, letting go.

He thought of Stephanie. Didn't they all?

Sebastian turned a corner to where the outpatient lab was located. But, delegating or not, his mother still insisted on going in every day for a short number of hours. They needed her, she'd insisted. Sebastian knew how important remaining vital was to a person's well-being. He couldn't take that away from her.

So the matter of whether to remain or leave had been settled without a single conversation. He'd made his mind up on his own as he left Stephanie's room yesterday.

Once he'd decided, his next task was to see Sheila Pollack and take her up on her offer before she changed her mind. He'd driven to her office, then, pulling into the parking lot, he'd taken out the card she'd given him and called her on his cell phone.

Sheila had still been enthusiastic. They met after six in her office. Sebastian discovered that the woman was exceptionally easy to talk to, and he found himself liking her easygoing manner. In a way, he imagined his own mother had been like her when she'd been Sheila's age: determined, energetic and dedicated.

In his mother's case, the dedication revolved around providing a good life for him. If she hadn't staked him, he wasn't sure if he could have paid for medical school. His mother had refused to take no for an answer when she'd offered the money to him.

"You're the only son I have. Who else am I going to spend the money on?"

When he'd said, "Yourself," she'd only laughed at him.

Now it was his turn to repay the debt.

So he'd made his commitment. He was going to be Sheila Pollack's partner in her medical practice, effective as soon as the papers were drawn up. He'd been impressed with the fact that the woman felt the handshake between them was no less important or binding than the papers that some corporate lawyer would draw up and pore over.

She'd also surprised him when she told him that the lawyer she was turning the papers over to was Stephanie's brother, Matthew.

Small world.

Maybe too small, he mused.

Sebastian tried to keep his mind uncluttered as he walked around the hospital, taking things in. This was a tour, pure and simple, he told himself. He wanted to completely familiarize himself with Harris Memorial's layout.

The last time he recalled being here, his mother had rushed him in for stitches after a major collision at third base. He stopped playing baseball shortly after that.

The hospital had changed a lot since then, built up, added on to. Sebastian soaked it all in. He liked knowing every inch of the terrain he was associated with.

Sebastian's thoughts drifted back to Matthew. He wondered if Matthew would find a tactful way to advise Sheila not to enter into a partnership with him. But turning his back on a doomed love affair wasn't in the same class as living up to the responsibilities of a medical practice partnership. Matthew was a fair man, he always had been. He wouldn't introduce something from his private life and use it against him.

Maybe having to deal with Matthew on something so clinical and removed as a medical practice partnership might bridge the gap that was between them, Sebastian thought. Maybe it would even restore a smattering of the friendship he'd lost.

Lost because he'd done the right thing, the noble thing. And cut his heart out in the process.

He missed them both, Sebastian thought. Matthew and Stephanie. They had been important parts of his life once. Before he told himself that he didn't need anyone.

He blinked as the elevator doors parted. Fifth floor. His mouth curved in a slight smile as he stepped out.

It seemed to him somehow fated that he would find himself getting off on the fifth floor. After all, Maternity would be where most of his practice would take him at all hours of the day and night.

He knew it was an excuse.

He'd purposely wandered to the fifth floor because Stephanie was here and he wanted to see her. Any noble intentions he'd had were now seven years in the past.

There was no harm in seeing her, he argued silently. No harm in seeing how she was doing. Nothing could come of it.

Knocking on the door, he waited for her response. When she didn't answer, he knocked again.

"Yes?"

That was all the invitation he figured he needed. Pushing open the door, he peered in.

"Hi, I was just in the neighborhood and wondered how you were doing tod—"

He stopped as the door slid closed behind him again. There was an open suitcase on Stephanie's rumpled bed. Fully dressed in street clothes, Stephanie was standing beside the bed, tossing things into the suitcase. The result was an unorganized jumble. Slippers were mated with a book and nestled against a robe whose sleeve was hanging out over the side. The flowers he'd brought had been moved to the table that ordinarily held her meal trays.

Sebastian looked from the suitcase to Stephanie. "You're checking out?" It seemed awfully soon to him. "Room service not to your liking?"

Surprised to hear his voice, she looked up and stopped packing for a beat before resuming. She hadn't expected him to come back again. Each time she saw him leave, she was prepared never to see him again. That way it wouldn't hurt the way it had before.

The nerve endings in her body came alive and stood at attention as he looked at her. She told herself this was stupid, that she had to stop reacting to him like this every time she saw him.

There's nothing there anymore, Stef. Do you hear me? It refused to sink in.

"Nothing wrong with room service," she quipped, her tone dead.

Because she wanted to keep her hands busy, she began folding items instead of just tossing them. Word had gone out, Matthew had seen to that. Her friends had stopped by, with wishes and gifts, most of which refused to fit into her suitcase. A nurse had given her a plastic shopping bag, but it was becoming full as well.

"Actually, the food's a lot better than I thought it would be." She placed two tiny embroidered, matching sweaters on top of her robe, wishing with all her heart that Brett and Holly could see the babies in them. "But it's time to start dealing with the rest of my life."

Funny, she'd had the same thought when Sebastian had left her—after crying an ocean of tears and thinking she was going to die from the pain in her heart.

She didn't trust herself to look at him just then. Hands on hips, she looked around the room to see if she'd missed something.

There was no indication, as far as Sebastian could see, that someone had recently occupied the room. "Who's taking you home?"

Stephanie felt herself growing defensive. "I am." She nodded at the telephone on the side. "And a cab service as soon as I call one."

His brow narrowed, surprised. "You mean no one's picking you up?"

Matthew had offered, but then had to cancel at the last minute. She knew her brother had assumed she'd ask someone else. But there were times Matthew didn't know her as well as he believed he did, she thought with a touch of amusement. She hadn't wanted to impose on anyone else. She wanted to be back in command of her life again.

"I'm a big girl, Sebastian," she told him. "I haven't needed to be picked up for quite some time now."

There was a time he would have taken offense at her tone. He let it slide. "Who's going to wheel you out to the curb?"

She stopped pretending that her packing was commanding all of her attention. "Excuse me?"

His mouth curved. He knew he'd caught her. "When they take you down, someone has to bring you out to the curb in a wheelchair."

There was nothing wrong with her legs. She'd given birth, not had a hip replacement. "I don't want to go out in a wheelchair."

"Hospital policy."

"Well, they can just go get a new policy." Stephanie tossed her head, sending her hair flying over her shoulder. She felt a little tired, maybe, but that was all. She'd be fine once she was seated in the cab with her children. "I'm walking out of here."

Entertained, he watched as her eyes flashed. "They won't let you."

The hell "they" wouldn't, Stephanie thought. "They can't stop me," she informed him defiantly. She'd bucked her father, she certainly wasn't going to be intimidated by some nurse trying to foist a wheelchair on her when she didn't need or want one.

He leaned over the table, until he was directly in her line of vision. "Maybe not, but I can."

That caught her off guard. Her eyes narrowed. "Why would you?"

"Because I'm part of the staff now," he told her mildly.

Suspicion clouded her eyes. "Since when?" she demanded.

"Since yesterday afternoon." He looked at her significantly. "Means I have to go along with the policies and not make waves."

He was the original rebel. That was part of what had attracted her to him in the first place. And part of what her father had disapproved of so stridently. "That'll be the day."

His smile was easy, laid-back and all the more infuriating because of it. "Only one I see making waves here is you right now."

She didn't have time to argue with him. The doctor would be by shortly to sign her out and then she'd do what she damn well pleased. Until then, there was no harm in letting him think she was giving in. "All right, I'll go down in a wheelchair."

He knew her too well to be taken in by the sudden docile behavior. "Then what?"

"Then I'll get out of the wheelchair." The frail hold on her temper loosened. "Did you come here just to annoy me?"

''Fringe benefit.'' God help him, he still loved seeing the fire that came into her eyes. It matched the fire he knew was in her soul. There'd been a time when he'd thought of himself as keeper of the flame. Showed how much he knew. ''I came to look the place over, get myself familiar with the different floors.''

A glint of triumph entered her eyes. She'd caught him in a lie. ''I thought you said you were an ob-gyn.''

He knew that look. Some things, he thought, hadn't changed. He found a certain comfort in that, though he knew he shouldn't. None of this would lead anywhere. It was too late. Too much time had passed. ''I am. Doesn't mean I have to be narrow-minded about it. An open mind is a healthy mind.''

His expression was serious. She wondered if it was for her benefit. ''You have changed, haven't you?''

A great deal, in some respects, he thought. He'd learned to relax a little, not to play things so close to the chest. But he still retained a great many of his old feelings. Especially about her.

''Not really, just not being so secretive about some things anymore.''

Before Stephanie could ask him what he meant by that, her doctor breezed into the room. Sheila smiled, surprised and pleased to see Sebastian there.

''So,'' she asked Stephanie as she picked up her chart, ''what do you think of my new partner?''

Too stunned to know whether or not she was dismayed, Stephanie could only stare at her doctor. "You're the medical firm he's joining?"

Sheila tried to decipher Stephanie's reaction. "I'll still be your doctor, Stephanie." She scanned the morning nurse's notes. "Any history you two have won't be a problem."

That's what you think. A vague sense of betrayal drifted through her. Stephanie pressed her lips together. What she thought of the new partnership had no bearing on its outcome.

"I wouldn't think so," she replied stiffly.

Sheila gave her a reassuring smile. She paused at the line that required her signature. "Still want to go home? Your insurance lets you stay until tomorrow, you know."

Stephanie shook her head. "No, I'm sure. I might as well get used to the routine."

Sheila laughed. "Take it from a mother, you *never* get used to the routine. And," she reiterated, though she had a feeling that Stephanie had made up her mind, "I'd strongly suggest you stay and take advantage of the rest. Trust me, this'll probably be the last time you'll have any long-term relationship with your pillow for the next year."

She had her own reasons for leaving the hospital and going home. "I'll take my chances."

"Brave lady." Sheila patted her shoulder. "Okay." She flipped the pages on the chart back to their original position and returned the chart to its holder against the bed. "You're free to go." She looked at Sebastian. "I take it you're here to take her home."

"Yes."

"No," Stephanie insisted.

"Multiple choice." Sheila laughed. "I always did like seeing those on exams. They always gave me an even chance of getting the right answer." She patted Sebastian's arm as she began to leave. "Drive carefully. You'll have precious cargo on board." Sheila stopped in the doorway, a thought hitting her. "Do you have two baby seats in the car or one?"

Sebastian looked meaningfully at her. Stephanie knew what he was thinking. That she couldn't possibly have baby seats if she was leaving by cab. And he'd be right.

Stephanie swallowed an oath. "I hadn't thought of that."

For that matter, she hadn't thought of how she would transport both babies home at the same time, either. Stephanie flushed, embarrassed. She'd just wanted to get out and go home.

"Not to worry," Sheila said brightly. "I'll see if we can fix you up with a couple of 'loaners' from the children's ward. Sebastian, come with me." She commandeered his arm, taking him with her. "Your education might as well start now. I'll show you where we keep our 'miscellaneous' things filed."

"All right, admit it."

Two nurses had accompanied them down in the

elevator, each holding a baby. Stephanie had remained silent the entire time. Her silence hadn't even broken once they were in the car and on their way.

She kept her face forward, looking at the road. Battling a growing queasy feeling in her stomach. *My God, what had she gone and done? Two babies. How was she ever going to survive?*

She was only half listening to him. "Admit what?"

He carefully guided the car along the road. It seemed to him that there was a great deal more traffic than usual. "Admit that it was a good thing for me to come along when I did."

She blew out a breath, knowing he was right. But knowing he was right didn't make it any easier to say the words. They lay heavily on her tongue. "I would have managed."

He laughed shortly. "You really are your father's daughter, aren't you?"

The remark incensed her. "That was a nasty thing to say."

Maybe, but that didn't change things. "He could never admit he was wrong, either."

She thought of the cold, granitelike expression that would come over her father's face when he didn't approve of something. There was no approaching him.

"No," she agreed, "he couldn't." She hated the thought that she was anything like Carlton Yarbourough. "All right, I was wrong. It was a good thing you came along when you did."

Satisfied, Sebastian decided to probe a little further into her world. Something was bothering him, something he wasn't about to put into words just yet. But he needed some information first before he could place it into perspective for himself. "Why didn't Matthew come?"

"He wanted to, but at the last minute, he got tied up in court. Something about a litigation running over. When he called from the courthouse to tell me, he said he'd come by the hospital this evening." She shrugged. "I didn't want to wait."

Turning in her seat, Stephanie leaned against her hand on the back of the seat and looked at the twins. The infants were strapped into small seats, housed side by side. Brett was dozing, but Holly was taking everything in. "I don't think I'll start thinking that all this is real until I actually have them home."

Holly began to fuss as they pulled into the driveway of the modest home Stephanie had pointed out to him as being hers.

Perfect timing, Sebastian thought. He pulled up the hand brake. "You might have wanted to rethink that," he suggested.

A bemused smile played on Stephanie's lips. "Too late now."

Part of her was looking forward to this and part of her was absolutely terrified at the prospect of being both mother and father to these two tiny human beings. There were so many questions she had, so many uncertainties facing her. About the only thing she did know was that she loved these little people who had come into her life, not unannounced but certainly unexpected.

She leaned against the car door handle just before opening it. "Well, since you're here, I guess you might as well make yourself useful and bring one of the babies in."

Amusement tugged at the corners of his mouth, melting away the years and making him look boyish. "Would you have ordered me around like this if I were the cab driver?"

She spared him a look before she swung her legs out of the car. "Yes."

He believed her and laughed.

Getting out, he saw Stephanie falter as she tried to gain her feet. He rounded the hood quickly, getting to her side in time to put his arms around her. "What's the matter?"

She tried to wave away his concern. "Nothing, I just got dizzy, that's all."

"Probably your stubbornness kicking you in the seat," he commented with feeling. Pocketing his car keys, he kept one arm around her waist. The contact stirred him, bringing back memories. "Put your arm around my neck. I'm going to carry you inside."

Still a tad woozy, she still refused to do what he told her. "Don't be ridiculous."

The woman would probably argue with God,

given half a chance. Seeing that both her father and her brother were lawyers, he figured she came by it naturally. Arguing was in her blood. "I'm being practical. I don't want you passing out."

"I'm not going to pass out," she insisted. She hated being treated as if she was fragile. "It's gone now, whatever it was. Besides, what about the babies?"

He looked at the duo. Brett was beginning to wake up. "Don't worry, I won't make them walk. They'll get their turn."

"You can't leave them in the car." She might not know much about being a mother, but she knew enough to at least know you didn't leave babies in cars.

"They're not old enough to drive, there's nothing to worry about," he quipped. He'd only meant to bring her into her living room before going to retrieve the twins. Since Stephanie was putting up a fuss, he tried to accommodate her. "Tell you what. I'll bring you in last. Sit here."

"I will not—"

His eyes narrowed as his tone grew firmer. "Sit."

The single-word command rankled her. "What do you think I am, a dog?"

"Absolutely not. A dog would be obedient."

Like flames igniting in a liberally greased frying pan, her temper flared. "Is that what you require in a woman, obedience?"

He was tired of arguing over everything. Releasing

her, he went to unstrap one of the twins. "Actually, what I require is common sense, something you apparently seemed to have pushed out along with the twins."

She opened her mouth to tell him exactly what she thought of his opinion, but her head began to spin again and she found herself sinking onto the seat, her hand clammy as she grasped the inside of the car to steady herself.

The world tilted out of sync before it receded to a black dot and then abruptly disappeared.

Chapter Seven

Her eyelids felt as if they each weighed a ton as she struggled to lift them.

It took Stephanie a moment before her eyes focused and engaged with her brain. Everything seemed foggy to her. She realized that she was flat on her back on the sofa in her living room, looking up at her ceiling.

There was something wet on her forehead. Reaching, her fingers came in contact with a cloth. A handkerchief, by the feel of it. It took effort just to drag the wet cloth off.

What had happened to her?

"Leave that where it is." Sebastian's voice materialized out of nowhere, cutting through the haze encircling her brain.

The next moment, she saw him, hovering over her. There was concern in his eyes. Something distant warmed within her.

Moving the handkerchief up farther, Stephanie dropped her hand to her side. That, too, felt unusually heavy. "What happened?"

"You came home too soon," he told her simply.

Everything came rushing back at her. She was outside, getting out of the car. The babies were in their borrowed car seats in the back.

The babies.

Alert, worried, she grasped the side of the sofa and tried to sit up. The handkerchief slid down onto her face. She threw it aside. "The babies...?"

With gentle firm hands on her shoulders, Sebastian pushed her back down, then replaced the handkerchief on her forehead. No longer cool, it still helped a little. "They're all right. They're in their bassinets."

The nursery was at the other end of the house. "Alone?"

His mouth curved. "The bassinets are too small for them to entertain guests." He saw the agitation in her eyes. He'd never doubted that she would make a good mother when her time came. "But don't worry, Iris is watching over them."

Slowly, her hold on the upholstery loosened. "Iris?"

"My mother's best friend," he explained. "A

grandmother seven times over, so I think they're in safe hands.''

He'd called his mother for the woman's phone number as soon as he'd gotten both Stephanie and the twins into the house. He had no idea if Stephanie had fainted, or if her condition was more serious, and until he assessed the situation, he needed someone to watch the babies. Iris Jorgansen had arrived within ten minutes of the call and taken the babies over.

There were times he could read Stephanie like a book. Like now. He could tell she wasn't entirely convinced. ''Part of being self-sufficient is knowing when you need help,'' he told her, his tone deceptively mild.

She needed help, all right, she thought, a wave of hopelessness washing over her. There was no denying that. But she couldn't seem to get her act together. Not since the accident had shattered everything.

Feeling a drop of water trickle down the side of her temple, she took off the wet cloth, wadding it in her hand. ''How long was I out?''

He took his handkerchief from her and tossed it on a pile of newspapers on the coffee table to dry. Sebastian sat down on one corner, facing her. ''Long enough for Iris to get here and change diapers. She's feeding them right now.''

''But I'm—that is—'' She could feel her face growing crimson.

It amused and amazed him that Stephanie had suddenly grown shy in front of him. Not because he'd delivered her babies, but because of the intimacy they'd once shared, physically and emotionally. He supposed it was only natural that some things had changed between them, but it wasn't easy getting used to it.

"Don't worry. The formula's just a temporary substitute." He allowed himself only a fleeting glance at her bustline. "You weren't exactly in any condition to breast-feed."

She flushed, unconsciously hunching her shoulders. "I'm all right now."

"No, you're not all right now," he insisted. He knew her, she'd push herself until she dropped. It was her nature. "I've got a degree to back up that opinion, you don't," he added sternly when she opened her mouth in protest. "Iris can stay for another couple of hours." He rose, knowing it wasn't safe to sit close to her like this for too long. Too many memories, too many urges hovered on the fringes of his consciousness, waiting for a chance to break through. To make him slip and give in to an impulse. "I'll be back before she's gone."

Propping herself up on her elbow, she found that the room insisted on moving with her. She struggled to stabilize it. "You?"

"Sure." He took no offense at the surprised tone in her voice. "I'll just throw together a few things and be back in a few hours."

Panic came out of nowhere, which she could only

attribute to misaligned hormones, thrown off by the process of giving birth. It wouldn't recede.

"Don't put yourself out. I can call a nanny service...."

Nothing Stephanie could say in protest, now that he knew she wasn't married or in a relationship, could dissuade him from lending a hand. If nothing else, then for old times' sake. At a different place and time, these babies he was helping her with could have been theirs.

"You're not exactly up to doing in-depth interviews right at the moment. Now, stay there." Sebastian leveled a stern look at her as he pointed to the sofa. "Doctor's orders."

The old fire returned to her eyes as she tossed her head. "You're not my doctor."

He placed a restraining hand on her shoulder, silently reinforcing his order. "In lieu of Sheila, I'll have to do. Besides, if you try to get up, Iris is instructed to sit on you and you really don't want that to happen. She's six-one and was an Olympic contender for the shot put back in 1952."

Coming around behind her, Sebastian adjusted the pillows and tucked in another one under her shoulders in an effort to make her as comfortable as possible.

Stephanie twisted around to look at him. She just didn't understand. It didn't make any sense. Seven years ago he'd walked out of her life, now Sebastian was behaving as if he was some old friend who'd dropped out of the sky. As if they didn't have a history that involved something much more.

"Why are you putting yourself out like this?"

"I told you—" he purposely kept his tone light "—I'm a friend."

She turned up her face to his as he moved forward. The look in her eyes triggered something within him, something that rushed up and caught him by the throat, taking his breath away. The next moment, before he realized what he was doing, he was leaning over her, brushing his lips against hers.

He caught himself just in time. Just before he had a chance to do it again, this time with more feeling. There was no doubt in his mind that all hell would break loose if he did.

"I'll see you in a couple of hours," he promised quietly.

Her heart pounding, her emotions more tangled than ancient tree roots, Stephanie stared at the front door long after he'd closed it behind him, trying desperately to catch hold of a thought and anchor it down.

She failed.

Good as his word, Sebastian returned in just under two hours. He'd thrown some things together into an overnight bag, explained the situation to his mother and reminded her of both his pager and his cell phone numbers should she need anything.

"I'm not a child, Sebastian," Geraldine had said,

laughing. "I can remember your cell phone number for more than one day at a time."

He'd kissed her goodbye, ignoring the pleased expression on her face. To her credit, his mother hadn't asked him any probing questions about either Stephanie or why he was volunteering to help her. The woman was one of a kind.

Stephanie's keys were still in his pocket and he used them now to unlock her front door. When he walked in, the first thing he saw was that the sofa was unoccupied.

"Damn it," he muttered under his breath, sliding the keys back into his pocket.

He supposed that he hadn't actually thought Stephanie would remain where he'd told her to, but under the circumstances, he had hoped...

The woman didn't have the sense she was born with, only the stubbornness, he thought, annoyed. She'd seen how weak she still was, how susceptible to fatigue. Would it have killed her to stay on the sofa the way he'd told her to and rest?

Apparently so.

He blew out a breath. He didn't need this.

"Iris?" he called out, striding through the living room and into the hall.

In response, the woman emerged at the far end from one of the bedrooms.

"Don't blame me," she said, second-guessing the reason for his tone. A wriggling Brett Yarbourough, all six pounds, two ounces of him, was lightly pressed against her shoulder. She patted his back with gentle, concentric circles. At sixty-seven and more than six feet tall, Iris Jorgansen had the face of an angel and the body of a skilled linebacker. The helpless shrug she gave him seemed completely incongruous with the shadow she cast. "I tried everything I could short of tying your friend up, but she refused to rest on the sofa or go to bed. Said she needed to feed the twins or she was going to explode."

Sebastian frowned at the flimsy excuse. It was a little soon for Stephanie to be as full as she claimed, especially since it was her first time. Efforts to the contrary, he'd taken note of that part of her anatomy. It hardly looked any larger than it ordinarily did.

Never having experienced the sensation himself, he supposed he had no choice but to let Stephanie and her excuse slide. But not without a few words.

"Where is she?"

Crossing to him, Iris nodded toward the room she'd just left.

"In the nursery. Working on the other one. Listen, I'd like to stay, but…"

Moving the infant to the crook of her arm, she handed Sebastian the folded cloth diaper that had been on her shoulder, then transferred the baby to him.

He took the small bundle into his arms. "Sure, I understand. You've been a godsend, Iris. I don't know what my mother or I would have done without you.''

The woman lit up at the compliment. ''Nothing like being appreciated to lift your spirits.'' She shook her head. ''My Henry never did get the knack of that. Thank God he didn't pass it on to any of the kids.'' She paused to look down at the baby she'd just surrendered to Sebastian. Her smile was utterly maternal. ''Little angels, both of them. Their mother's a firebrand, though.'' She picked up her purse from the floor where she had left it and slipped the strap onto her shoulder. ''You're going to have your hands full with that one.''

He had a feeling that Iris had misconstrued the situation that currently existed between Stephanie and him, but he let it pass. It would take too long to clarify and he had no desire to go into details. ''Tell me something I don't know.''

Pausing to look in the mirror that hung over the side table on the wall and pat her hair into place, Iris looked at his reflection over her shoulder.

''All right, I will.'' Their eyes met in the mirror. ''Beneath all that fire is a scared girl. Be gentle with her.''

''Got the kid gloves right here in my pocket,'' he assured her.

Turning around again, Iris laughed, the room rocking with the booming noise. ''I'll stop by your mother's on my way home.''

Sebastian walked her to the door. "I appreciate it, Iris."

Iris waved away his thanks. "No need to thank me." She leaned over the baby. "Goodbye, Brett," she cooed, then left.

"Let's go find your mom," he said to Brett. The baby stared at him with wide blue eyes. Like Stephanie's, he thought. "Glad we're in agreement here."

He ventured into the rear bedroom at the end of the long corridor slowly. Intended to be a study, the room had hastily been turned into a nursery at the last minute. A hybrid of both, it was neither. There were uneven towers of books scattered all along the floor, forming what amounted to a semicircle around two bassinets, a changing table and a rocking chair.

He found Stephanie in the rocking chair, her eyes drooping as she held the suckling infant to her breast. Because the urge to simply stand there, drinking in the scene was so great, Sebastian cleared his throat, gaining her attention. Sleep faded the instant she saw him entering the room.

"You're back." Belatedly, Stephanie moved the baby's blanket up a little higher on her breast to cover herself.

Purposely averting his eyes, Sebastian looked at her face. "I said I would be." Very carefully, he placed Brett into his bassinet. "What are you doing up?"

It had been a long time since she'd had to explain

her actions to anyone and she didn't like it. "I had to feed the babies."

"I told you, there's formula for that. The hospital packed it in an 'emergency kit' of sorts for panicking young mothers."

The remark grated on her already raw nerves. "I'm not a panicking young mother and I don't want the babies getting used to formula."

They were arguing about nonsense. The bottom line was her stubborn resistance to taking it easy for another day. And her even more stubborn resistance to accepting any advice, especially from him.

Playing dirty, he pulled off the kid gloves he'd joked about and hit her where he knew it would be the most effective.

"They've already lost two parents, you're the only spare they have. Don't you think you should take care of yourself a little better?"

He was right. Again. She didn't know which she resented more. That he was right, or that he was here, in her space, messing with her mind. And stirring up emotions she'd tried so hard to bury.

"I take vitamins," she said defensively. "That's what I was doing when you saw me in the parking lot, getting my prescription filled."

He reached for the baby still in her arms. Stephanie looked down at the tiny face and saw that Holly had fallen asleep. Very gently, she moved her nipple out of the rosebud mouth.

For a second, his breath caught in his throat. Sebastian felt everything within him tighten as he watched the simple, intimate scene. With superhuman effort, he banked down his feelings. There was no place for that here.

He kept repeating that to himself as he gently placed the infant against his shoulder. Almost automatically, he began to pat the small back, waiting for a tiny burp. "Vitamins can't do anything if you're too tired to take them."

There was a gentleness to Sebastian that she couldn't remember witnessing before. It tugged at her heart and Stephanie upbraided herself for the soft feelings floating through her. This was the man who'd left her. The man who hadn't tried a single time to get in contact with her. She had to remember that.

Her eyes narrowed. "Since when did you turn into a worrywart?"

Sebastian heard the small telltale noise that sounded suspiciously like a burp. Pleased, he placed Holly into her bassinet and lightly covered the infant. He raised his eyes to Stephanie's and saw that she was watching him, a strange expression on her face.

"That's Dr. Worrywart, thank you." He succeeded in coaxing a smile, albeit a small one, out of her. "There, that's better."

"I don't know what you're talking about," she informed him with a sniff. Stephanie gripped both armrests on the rocker for leverage as she tried to stand up.

The next moment, instead of standing, she found herself being swept up into his arms. His big, muscular, strong arms. She told herself not to enjoy it. But it was hard to listen when her heart was pounding so loudly in her ears.

Still, she tried her best to look annoyed, even as she slipped her arms around his neck. "What do you think you're doing?"

"Taking you to bed."

The answer had her pulse quickening until she realized he meant that in the sense that it was a location, not an activity that stretched ahead of them, as it once had. "But I haven't eaten yet—"

He glanced at the baby monitor and saw that it was on. Sebastian eased out of the room, then quietly closed the door with his fingertips. "I'll bring you a tray."

"You cook?" His upbringing in the back of a restaurant notwithstanding, the last she remembered, he had needed a diagram to make a sandwich.

"Passably." A man couldn't live on his own for seven years and not learn how to prepare some things. "But my mother sent over a chicken-and-broccoli casserole for you."

The fond feeling brought a stab of guilt in its wake. After his mother wouldn't tell her where Sebastian had gone, she'd purposely lost touch with the woman because the contact had been too much of a reminder of the disappointment she'd suffered. Geraldine Caine hadn't been to blame for her son's thoughtlessness.

Stephanie flushed. "Your mother knows you're staying here?"

He had no idea what brought the pink hue to her cheeks, but he knew better than to ask. "I make it a point never to lie, and I wanted her to know where to find me if she needed me."

He might not lie outright, but he'd lied to her, Stephanie thought. Lied when he said he'd always be there for her. That he'd always love her.

Self-preservation struggled to regain its hold on her. She couldn't let herself forgive him, couldn't allow herself to become vulnerable again and go through what she had before.

"You know, there's no need for you to stay."

She was blowing cool again. He could hear it in her voice. "You're not feeling well and I don't want you on my conscience."

Her expression was grim as she looked at him. "I wasn't aware you still had one." She saw his jaw grow rigid and knew he was struggling not to retort. "Sorry, low blow," she muttered.

His eyes met hers. "Yes, it was."

She refused to back down, despite the minor apology. "But you deserved it."

"Maybe."

And maybe, someday, she would understand that he had done it for her, not himself. That if he'd had the choice and could have made it with a clear conscience, she would have been his wife these last seven years. But what kind of a life would that have been for her? She might have visited the other side, but she really had no comprehension of how the other half lived. Or what it meant to live that way, to do without.

Bringing her into her room, Sebastian set her down on the bed. Stephanie didn't immediately release her arms from around his neck. His eyes looked into hers for a long moment. Without being fully aware of it, he slowly swept his fingertips along her cheek.

The next thing he knew, he was gathering her into his arms and kissing her. Kissing her because the ache within him refused to fade away, refused to abate and demanded some sort of tribute.

The small, fleeting kiss he'd brushed against her lips earlier had whet his appetite and his memory, not giving him peace. It had been so long, so very long, since he had held her in his arms like this. Since he had kissed her like this.

It was as if he had no control over his own actions, no ability to stop himself. The bittersweet taste he found on Stephanie's lips only intensified his reaction, intensified the need he felt laying claim to every fiber of his being.

He'd missed her more than he thought was humanly possible to miss anyone or anything. There'd been times when he told himself he was over her, times when he actually went from one end of a day to the other without longing for her. Even times when he'd gone for an entire day without thinking about her.

But the thoughts, the longings, the ache would always return to haunt him. Sometimes darkly, sometimes lightly, but always, always, they would return.

This was completely insane. She should be yelling at him, pushing him away, telling him what a louse she thought he was for abandoning her the way he had. But all the words she used to upbraid herself, to remind herself of how shabbily he'd ultimately treated her did no good, had no effect over the tidal wave of emotion sweeping over her. Sweeping her away.

He still wanted her.

She could taste it on his lips, feel it in his body. It wasn't exhaustion deceiving her. Sebastian still cared about her, still wanted her.

It helped assuage some of the pain.

But not all of it.

Abruptly, she loosened her arms from his neck and drew away.

"Maybe I'd better get that tray for you," he suggested.

"Maybe," she agreed quietly, annoyed with the way her whole body had suddenly come alive. The way it was throbbing now, despite her condition, despite the very real hurt that still reigned within her.

As he left the room, she sank back against the pillow and told herself not to cry.

Chapter Eight

Stephanie was on automatic pilot.

There was no other way to say it, he thought as he drove toward her house. Incredibly healthy, Stephanie did what needed to be done.

Still, over her protests, he'd taken to dropping by with groceries, takeout or an occasional toy for the twins. It had begun as a temporary thing. He hadn't meant it to be any more than a couple of days at most.

But somehow, a "couple of days" had knit themselves into several, and now he'd been dropping by every day, including weekends, for the last three weeks.

She'd gotten used to him appearing on her doorstep after six, he could tell. The protests were murmured for form's sake. He had even begun to get the feeling that she didn't mind him coming. He'd observed her and there'd been a definite change. He wasn't all that sure it was for the better, but after he'd left to get her something to eat that first day, she'd undergone a transformation. When he'd returned with her dinner, it was as if she'd managed to get a superhuman grip on herself.

Any spark, any indication that there had been something between them, that there still *was* something, however small, between them, was gone. Wiped away. In its place was a look of sheer determination, belonging to a woman who had her mind singularly focused on coping, on making it through this new maze she'd suddenly discovered herself inhabiting.

She was, he had to admit, amazing. That was it in a nutshell. He had no idea what had happened in those few minutes she'd been by herself, while the taste of her kiss had still lingered on his lips, but she'd changed. Changed almost radically. She even ceased looking tired. It was as if determination had blotted out everything in its wake. Including him.

Oh, she still talked to him, but her words seemed as if they were addressed to a stranger, someone she might meet in passing. Not someone she'd had a history with.

He figured it was all for the best. They both needed to get past this point, to get over any residual feelings that might still be there. They were no longer the people they'd been seven years ago.

And yet...

There was no "and yet." This was the way things were supposed to be, he told himself, getting off the freeway and turning left.

Damn it, if she could suddenly revert to nothing short of an all-purpose, efficient android, he certainly could stop letting his mind dwell on the past again.

Couldn't he?

Sebastian sighed, waiting for the light to turn green. He should have known this was going to happen when he'd decided to come back home. He *had* known, he thought. But he'd made up his mind to deal with it. He'd actually thought he could. After all, he'd dealt with it for seven years.

But that had been before he'd seen her.

Still, it shouldn't have made that much of a difference to him. God knew he had enough on his mind, what with overseeing his mother's medical care. There were specialists to see and therapy sessions to arrange, not to mention that she insisted on going into the restaurant a few hours each day. He knew that was good, even though it tired her. She needed to feel necessary. The restaurant was almost as important to her as he was.

Besides all that, he was busy getting entrenched within Sheila Pollack's medical practice. That alone took more than a healthy bite out of his day. Sheila had been right about the growing roster of patients.

If anything, she had understated the number that came into her office in a day. And it seemed as if every second patient was either pregnant, or trying to become pregnant. In the last three weeks, he had already subbed for Sheila twice, delivering boys both times.

That didn't leave him a whole lot of time to play Good Samaritan. Not if he wanted to get any sleep.

He figured he'd catch up on his sleep in his forties.

Sebastian turned down another street. Traffic was moving particularly slowly. Which seemed par for the course since he was in a hurry to get to Stephanie's this evening.

At least his bringing Iris into her life had been the right thing to do, he thought. Rather than hire a nanny through a regular agency, Stephanie had taken it upon herself to talk Iris into taking on the responsibility for her part-time. That was all she needed, someone to pick up the slack a little.

With Iris on the job, there seemed little to no reason for him to continue stopping by on his way home from the office.

So why did he keep doing it?

Well, at least today he had a legitimate reason. Two, actually, if he factored in the disturbing detail about her father. He wasn't sure whether or not to tell her yet. But he knew he was going to read her the riot act for not showing up at her appointment. She had a two-thirty routine checkup with Sheila that she'd already postponed once because Holly looked as if she had colic. It had turned out to be only gas. But she had called the day before to cancel.

This time, there'd been no phone call of any kind, not even one after the fact. It wasn't like Stephanie. It was all he could do not to ask Sheila for some personal time and drive over to see what was wrong.

He turned into Stephanie's development and followed the zigzag path of streets feeding into one another until he reached her block. Hers was the last house on the left in the cul-de-sac.

Pulling up in the driveway, he noted that Iris's vintage tan Volvo station wagon was nowhere in sight. Because the office had been teeming with patients, two of whom were last-minute squeeze-ins, he was a little later than usual tonight. But Iris didn't normally leave until after he did. He'd secretly thought that Stephanie asked her to stay to act as a buffer to prevent anything from happening, the way it had the first day.

Was something up, or were these just all coincidences that had nothing to do with one another?

Sebastian rang the bell and waited. Then rang it again when there was no answer. By the time he rang a third time, he started getting concerned. Taking out his cell phone, he pressed the buttons for Stephanie's home phone. The telephone on the other end rang five times before the answering machine finally picked up.

Sebastian swallowed a curse. Frustrated, concerned, he fidgeted restlessly inside as he waited until the brief, succinct prerecorded message was over. "Stevi, it's me. If you're around, pick up. You're getting me worried. Pick up, Stevi…."

There was only silence.

Disgusted, he was about to flip his phone shut when he heard her voice on the other end. "Hello, Sebastian?"

It took him a second to realize that the voice coming from his cell phone belonged to Stephanie. It sounded hoarse and was barely audible. Concern went up several notches.

He placed the phone to his ear. "Stevi, open the door," he ordered. If she was inside, why hadn't she answered? He'd rung the bell long enough. "I'm right outside."

"Go away."

There was anger in her voice. Now he knew something was wrong. "Stevi, if you don't open the door, I'm going to break in through a window," he warned. He wished he hadn't given her back her keys. It would have made life a lot simpler now.

The connection was broken. She'd hung up. Swallowing another curse and battling a fear that had crept out of the shadows, Sebastian turned on his heel and started for his car. There was a tire iron in the trunk he could use to break the windowpane.

He heard the sound of the front door lock being flipped behind him. Sebastian swung around and was back on the front step before the door had finished opening.

Stephanie looked like hell. Her eyes were swollen and her hair hung in her face. She reminded him of someone who had been run over by defeat.

She made him think of the way he'd looked the morning after he'd left Bedford. And her.

She was barring the way into her house with her body. As if that would work. With a shake of his head, Sebastian simply moved her aside and entered. He masked his concern with anger. It was safer that way.

"Stevi, what the hell is going on?" he demanded. "You don't show up for your appointment, you don't answer your door—" He looked around, thinking that perhaps his mother's friend had parked her car in the garage. "Where's Iris?"

She waved a hand in the air, afraid she was going to break down in front of him. She didn't want him to see her crying, didn't want any displays of token pity. "I sent her home."

Nothing seemed out of the ordinary, at least out here. She wasn't making any sense. He pinned her with a look. "Why?"

Why was he badgering her? "Because I wanted to be alone," she snapped. "Something you don't seem to understand."

With effort, he kept his own temper in check. She was lashing out at him and he needed to know why. He started small. "Why did you break your appointment?"

She turned away from him, afraid he'd read the

truth in her eyes. More afraid she would break down. "I didn't feel like going in. It was only a routine checkup," she pointed out hotly. What was the big deal? Why was he so concerned? He hadn't been concerned about her when she needed him. Why now? "It'll keep."

Sebastian tried to get a good look at her. Stephanie tried to turn away, but he caught her shoulders and held her in place.

The android had broken down, he thought. There were tracks of tears, not yet dry, down her cheeks. "You've been crying."

Damn it, she wasn't going to be grilled this way. Her feelings were her own.

"No, I haven't," she retorted defiantly. "My eyes are just red. I didn't get much sleep last night, if it's any business of yours."

He'd never seen her like this.

Normally, he turned away from a show of temper, finding it easier to ignore the person until the tirade was over. But this wasn't any mood swing on Stephanie's part. Something was definitely wrong and he meant to get to the bottom of it.

His voice was as calm as hers was turbulent. "What's going on, Stevi?"

"Nothing," she insisted, shouting at him. "Can't you get it through your thick head that I want you to go away and leave me alone?" Momentum and near-hysteria began to build. "That I've got enough to deal with without you sticking your head in here every day, playing make-believe Daddy...?''

Sebastian discovered that the thick skin he'd grown had a crack in it. Stephanie's words had struck a nerve and it took effort for him not to defensively lash out at her, or just turn around and leave. But she needed him and he wasn't about to leave her.

''I'm not playing make-believe anything,'' he told her calmly. ''I'm your friend, Stevi—''

Fire came into her eyes. ''The hell you are.''

Friends didn't abandon friends, not after they'd promised to love them forever. But what was the use of saying that? It didn't change anything, help anything.

Taking a breath, she squared her shoulders. She needed to be alone, to think. ''Look, if you're doing this to soothe some guilty conscience, don't. Don't feel guilty. I absolve you of any guilt,'' she told him, sarcasm weighing down her words. Weary, she hardly recognized herself. But she'd been pushed to the limit and she was afraid that she didn't have time for niceties. ''Now, get the hell out of my house and out of my life.''

When Sebastian remained standing there, the last of her composure fell apart. She surprised him by slamming the heels of both palms against his chest and pushing him back.

''I want you to leave me alone.'' She hit him again, trying to make him go. ''Damn you, what part of 'leave me alone' don't you understand?''

He caught her wrists and stopped her from making contact a third time. As he sublimated both his concern and his anger, there was only kindness in his eyes as he looked at her.

"You can rant and rave all you want, Stevi. You're not going to push me away until I know what's going on." His grip tightened as she tried to pull her hands away. "This isn't like you."

"How do you know what's 'like' me?" she demanded. "You've been gone for seven years. You can't just waltz back into my life and expect to be on top of things—or me—just like that." Stephanie tossed her head. "I had a life after you left—"

"I know that." There was no emotion in his voice. "I delivered part of it three weeks ago."

Unable to hold herself in check any longer, Stephanie raised her voice and screamed at him. "So go, leave me alone! Go be a good doctor or a good son or a good whatever-you-want and just get out of here. Get out of here!" she repeated, her voice cracking.

Whatever had set her off was going to break her apart if he left, he knew that.

Sebastian folded his arms around her. "I'm not going anywhere, Stevi," he told her softly.

She could have continued mustering her anger against him if he'd been cold, or nasty, or if he'd raised his voice and shouted at her. But she couldn't handle kindness. It burrowed straight for her vulnerability and made her dissolve into tears right in front of him.

She hated her reaction, hated this display of weakness, but she couldn't seem to help herself.

Cold fear washed over him. Stephanie had him really scared now. In all the time he'd known her, he'd never seen her cry. She'd come close a couple of times, when talking about her father, but there'd been something within her that refused to allow herself to break down.

Whatever it was was gone now.

He picked her up in his arms and carried her to the sofa. Sitting down with her on his lap, he held Stephanie as she cried it all out. His chest ached as she sobbed against it.

Rocking slightly, Sebastian stroked her hair, saying nothing. Knowing there was nothing he could say that would help until she was ready. He had no idea if this sudden outpouring was just a reaction to having held in all her emotions so rigidly these last few weeks, or if it had something to do with what he'd found out about her father. Did she know? Or was something else to blame? He figured she'd tell him soon enough.

For now, what Stephanie needed most, he knew, was someone just to hold her. So he did.

She cried for a long time.

And then, just as suddenly as she'd begun, she stopped.

Spent, Stephanie straightened up and wiped away one damp area with the back of her hand.

He pretended not to notice the embarrassed flush

on her cheeks as he dug into his pocket and pulled out a handkerchief. Sebastian wiped away the tears first on one cheek, and then the other, before offering her the handkerchief.

She took it, completing the job. Feeling foolish for letting him see her this way. "Why are you being so nice to me?"

More than anything, he wanted to kiss her, to make it all better. He knew that kissing her would only do the opposite. Her life appeared to already be tangled up enough.

"Maybe because I don't believe in kicking someone when they're down." He decided to start small and hopefully work his way up. "Why did you break your appointment to Dr. Pollack this afternoon?"

She sighed, drained. Almost as weary as when she'd given birth. Maybe even more so. "I didn't have the strength to come in."

He knew it. Sebastian scowled. "Damn it, Stevi, I told you not to overdo things in the beginning—"

"No." Stephanie shook her head, placing her fingertips against his lips to silence him. She couldn't bear to hear him berate her. "It's not that. I got a letter today...."

Very slowly, he moved her fingers from his lips. His eyes were on hers. "What kind of a letter?"

Instead of telling him, she dragged herself from his lap and then crossed to the small desk in the corner. There was only one thing on it, a wadded-up sheet of stationery. Picking it up, Stephanie smoothed it out and brought it over to Sebastian.

Beneath the wavy wrinkles was a letter from Janice Collier. He read the name and raised a brow, trying to make a connection. "Janice Collier, any relation to Brett?"

Stephanie swallowed, afraid she would cry all over again. This wasn't fair. First Holly and Brett and now the babies. It just wasn't fair. She bit her lip. "His mother."

Alerted, he had a feeling he knew what was coming. Sebastian scanned the letter, reading it quickly. "She wants the babies," he said unnecessarily as he let the letter drop on the sofa. He understood now. Stephanie was riding an emotional roller coaster; this was the proverbial last straw. "Legally—"

She didn't want to hear what he was going to say. Stephanie suddenly seemed to galvanize right in front of his eyes.

"I know all about 'legally.' I've heard 'legally' bandied about all my life." Her father was a famous, clever, sharp lawyer. But that didn't make the causes he championed right. She'd learned that early in life. "The law is a tool to be used. The side that has the best toolmaster, wins."

Her heart filled her throat. She pressed her lips together. "Sebastian, I made a promise to Holly on her deathbed that I wouldn't let her mother-in-law have the babies." Janice Collier was a rich, influential woman. She knew what she was going to be up against. "Just because a person's well-off doesn't mean that she's fit to be a parent." She thought back to the stories Holly had shared with her. Stories Brett had told her about his childhood. It was far from pretty. The woman had been emotionally abusive. "Brett's mother put him through hell while he was growing up. It made my life seem like a picnic. If it hadn't been for Holly and her love, I don't know what would have happened to Brett."

Just as Sebastian had been her salvation—at least for a little while, she thought sadly.

"I can't let that woman have Holly and Brett's babies. Besides—" she could feel fresh tears threatening to fall "—I love them. They're part of me, not just physically, but—" Her voice broke.

He rose and gathered her in his arms once more.

"I know," he told her quietly. "I know."

The bond between a mother and the children she gave birth to was strong. It had been there right from the start with Stephanie. There had been no adjustment, no threat of any sort of postpartum depression or alienation from the infants. There had been love in her eyes from the first moment. No one had to tell him that.

Sebastian held her for a long moment, waiting for her to get hold of herself again. When she did, he asked, "So, what are you going to do?"

She moved back from the shelter of his arms, even though she wanted to remain there. "What can I do? I'm going to fight her."

It seemed to be the only logical thing to do, given how she felt. "You're going to need a good lawyer."

Stephanie stiffened. She knew where he was going with this. "I'm not going to ask my father."

He could understand her reluctance, but it was the smartest course open to her. "It pains me to say this, but he is the best."

Her eyes darkened. He *would* praise her father, given the arrangement that had been between them, she thought. But that didn't change things for her. "I'm not going to give him the opportunity to turn me down."

Sebastian thought of the information he'd obtained, going through certain records. People changed when confronted with life-altering events. "He might surprise you. You are his flesh and blood."

Carlton Yarbourough had never once treated her like a loving father, never once shown her any love or compassion. And she would always remember that he had taken exceptional joy telling her that he had been able to buy Sebastian off. She tried not to think about that, not to hate her father and Sebastian.

"That never seemed to matter while I was growing up," she said coldly. "Besides, we haven't spoken for a long time."

He'd had a feeling there'd been a rift. "That would explain why you wouldn't know."

She looked at him, confused. What was he talking about? "Know what?"

He backtracked a little in order to fill her in. "The afternoon you checked out of the hospital, you said that Matthew was supposed to pick you up, but he canceled out at the last minute."

She knew that, she'd told him. "Right, he was involved in a litigation that ran over—"

Sebastian shook his head. "There was no litigation. Matthew was at the hospital with your father."

She'd spoken to Matthew just yesterday. He'd tried to talk to her again about giving the twins up for adoption. There'd been no mention of their father. "What are you talking about?"

"When I went with Sheila to get the car seats for the twins, I thought I saw Matthew and your father in the corridor, going into the MRI office. I've been busy, but I finally got a chance to do a little nosing around through the hospital records—"

She frowned. "Aren't they supposed to be confidential?" Not that rules had ever stopped him, she recalled.

He gave a noncommittal shrug. "Yes." He paused, then said, "Matthew accompanied your father to the hospital for some tests."

She'd never known her father to see a doctor in his life. He referred to them en masse as quacks. "What kind of tests?"

He knew the medical terms wouldn't mean anything to her. "Blood work and a series of bone scans."

There was bad blood between them, and more than

a few hot words, both his and hers. But he was still her father and something within her felt frightened for him. "What's wrong with my father?"

"I don't know," Sebastian told her. The tests he'd seen had all pointed to something terminal, but that information should be shared between her and her father. Or at least her family. She needed to hear it from one of them before she heard it from him. If her father, or her brother, wouldn't tell her, then he would. But first he had to try to see if he could set up the lines of communication. "But you can ask Matthew."

She was already at the telephone, dialing her brother's personal number.

Chapter Nine

Matthew was still in his office.

Raising her voice, Stephanie bullied her way past her brother's secretary on the telephone, demanding to speak to him. Sebastian debated taking the receiver out of her hand and hanging it up, but he figured that she needed to get this out of her system. He knew what it was like to worry about someone who was important to him.

Stephanie's body stiffened when she heard the telephone on the other end being picked up. "Matthew, it's Stephanie."

"Hi, Stef." She heard someone talking to him in the background. "I can't talk right now—"

She wasn't about to be put off, not after what Sebastian had just told her. "You damn well can *too* talk right now. What's going on, Matthew?"

His tone was guarded. "What do you mean?"

"With Father." Carlton Yarbourough had never been "Dad," or called by any other shortened form of endearment referring to his place in their lives. He had always been "Father." The name was formal, distant. It suited him. "And I want the truth."

She heard her brother blow out a frustrated breath. "You weren't supposed to know."

Then it was bad, she thought. Something inside of her sank. "Know what? What's wrong with him, Matthew? Why is Father having tests done at the hospital—and before you try to deny it, Sebastian saw him going into the MRI office."

For a moment there was silence on the other end of the line, as if Matthew was weighing his options. "He's got bone cancer, Stef. It's eating away at him. The progression is slow, but—"

"Bone cancer." Stephanie's mouth felt leaden as she repeated the diagnosis. Somehow, she'd never really thought of her father as being mortal before. Her hands tightened around the receiver, squeezing it. "How long have you known?"

"*Suspected.*" Matthew was quick to clarify the difference. "I didn't really have facts to base it on, but—"

It took effort to control her temper. "Don't play lawyer with me, Matt. How long?"

"Six months." Matthew said the two words as if he was testing each out before uttering them.

"Six months?" She felt betrayed, shut out. How could they have kept this from her? How could Matthew not have told her? "You knew he had bone cancer for the last six months and you didn't tell me?"

"We didn't know for sure and he swore me to secrecy," Matthew told her quickly. "He wouldn't have even told me except I was there one day when he just...collapsed." There was no better way to say it.

There was a sob suddenly forming in her throat. She did her best to keep it back. Six months. She sank onto the sofa, her knees unable to support her. "My God, Matthew. You should have told me."

Ever the peacemaker, Matthew felt his loyalties divided between the man he'd given his word to and the sister he loved. "He has a right to his dignity, Stephanie."

That was garbage and Matthew knew it, she thought hotly. You needed your family when you were ill. You needed your family to *know* you were ill. "What kind of dignity is there in being alone?"

Confronted with the cold anger he heard in her voice, Matthew fumbled before his sister the way he never did in court. They were a great deal alike, she and their father, he thought. "The two of you aren't speaking to each other—"

"And you didn't think that this would make a difference?'' She shook her head, stunned. Deliberately avoided looking toward Sebastian. ''Don't you know me at all, Matthew?''

He could only tell her the way it was. ''He didn't want it to make a difference.''

''Well, he can't always have what he wants, now, can he?'' Sarcasm dripped from her voice. Even in this, what should have been her father's time of need, he was shutting her out. And Matthew, Matthew should have known better. Her emotions raw, she didn't trust herself to speak to him. ''I'll talk to you later.'' She hung up before he could respond.

Sebastian could guess at Matthew's side of the conversation. ''You were a little hard on him, don't you think?''

Hard on him? She hadn't been hard enough. Getting off the sofa, she glared at Sebastian. ''What, you've suddenly decided to become the champion for the males in my family?''

He rose to his feet and stood in front of her. ''I'm not championing anything. The secret wasn't Matthew's to tell.''

''No, you're dead wrong there. It wasn't his to keep,'' she corrected him angrily. An impotence dragged at her, pulling her down. She wanted to hit something, to punch it until her knuckles were sore. ''Not when it's something like this.''

She could be stubborner than anyone he knew. ''Must be nice to be so convinced you're always right. Have you ever been wrong?''

Silence draped the room as she looked at him for a long moment. "Yes. Once."

And it had been about him, Sebastian thought. But she hadn't been, not where it counted. He'd loved her. Love had been the reason he'd left. He wanted to tell her that, to make her understand why he hadn't married her when he said he would. But that would be opening up wounds he had no intention of restitching. There was no point.

And at the bottom of it all, the initial reasons were still true. He was still the boy who had been born on the wrong side of the tracks and she was the princess he'd fallen in love with. People like that only got together in children's fairy tales.

Restless, feeling as if she was going to explode at any minute, Stephanie knew she couldn't remain here. "Can you do me a favor?" she asked suddenly.

Normally, to her, he would have said yes. But he didn't like the look he saw in her eyes. She looked overwrought. "What is it?"

"Can you stay with the twins for a while?" Assuming his agreement, she was already walking to where she kept her purse.

He matched her step for step. "Why, where are you going?"

"I'm going to see my father—"

Sebastian moved so that he blocked her access to the closet. "I don't think you're in any condition to go running off like this."

Her eyes darkened. "I don't remember asking you for your opinion."

"Consider it a freebie." The light tone left his voice. He looked at her pointedly. "You're not going anywhere tonight."

The anger she'd tried to suppress moments earlier flared. Who the hell did he think he was, giving her orders?

"You can't tell me what to do." She began to push past him to reach the closet and her purse.

He caught her arm, keeping her in place. "Oh, yes, I can. I'm a doctor, I don't walk away from the scene of an accident."

She had no idea what he was talking about. "There's no accident."

She yanked her arm away, but he placed his hands on her shoulders. There was no way he was going to let her leave in this condition.

"There will be if you go driving off half cocked like this. You've just had two bad shocks in a row. You need to put this on the back burner for the night and think it through. Otherwise you might say something you're going to regret later." He moved her back to the sofa. "Now, sit down and I'll draw you a hot bath."

Her chin shot up defiantly. She wasn't about to let him boss her around like this. "I don't need you to draw me a hot anything."

"Yes," he said firmly, "you do. You need to calm down and get a hold of yourself or you're not going to do the twins, your father or yourself any good, do you understand?''

Stephanie let out a long, impatient breath. ''You're a bully, you know that?''

He allowed a small smile to creep out onto his lips. ''I've been told that, yes.''

''And I could just plow right by you and leave.'' She was fairly certain he wouldn't use physical force to make her stay and she knew he wouldn't walk out and leave the twins alone.

Arching a brow, he looked at her pointedly. ''You could try.''

Her certainty dissolved. Stephanie sighed, giving up. If she went now, odds were her temper would get the better of her. Shouting at her father and telling him what she thought of him wasn't going to resolve anything. ''Maybe you're right.''

''I'm the doctor.'' Hands still on her shoulders, he pushed her down until she was sitting on the sofa. ''Of course I'm right.''

He really wasn't going to draw her a bath—was he? ''I don't need a bath—'' she protested

Sebastian stopped to look over his shoulder. ''Yes, you do. That's nonnegotiable. The hotter the better. If ever someone needed to unwind before they sprang out of control, it's you.''

She opened her mouth in protest as he walked out of the room, then shut it again.

Maybe, just this one time, she'd let the reins slip away from her fingers. Maybe, just this once, she'd let someone else take charge for a little while. The idea of a hot bath did sound pretty good right about now, she thought. And God knew she needed to unwind. She was tense enough to crack apart into tiny pieces.

She gave him five minutes, then went to see if he was actually filling the bathtub for her. Somehow, she couldn't see the old Sebastian doing that.

But this wasn't the old Sebastian. The old Sebastian would have lost patience with her and walked out instead of holding on to his temper and negotiating.

Bullying, she corrected.

Amusement tugged at her mouth.

The sound of rushing water grew louder as she walked into her bedroom. As did the sound of crying.

Standing in her doorway, Stephanie turned and looked over her shoulder toward the revamped study. Thanks to Sebastian's efforts and the baby shower gifts Holly and Brett had received, the room was almost entirely a nursery now. One of the twins was awake and making itself heard. The other one would be awake, too, in a matter of seconds. So much for the bath.

She started to leave, but Sebastian caught up with her and took hold of her hand. He drew her back into her room.

"I'll take care of him."

She knew she should protest, but she was suddenly too weary. She needed to revitalize more than she needed to win a minor skirmish quickly forgotten. "How do you know it's a him?"

Sebastian winked at her. "Men are lighter sleepers." He pointed toward the bathroom. "You just get in there and start soaking. And I don't want to see you come out until you're completely pruney and your mind is entirely empty."

That was a tall order. "Did you bring a change of clothing with you?" she deadpanned.

He grinned, gently pushing her toward the bathroom. "Just get in there."

Stephanie sighed. Her breath lifted a precarious soap sud, carrying it away. She watched it sink back to the water.

He was right again.

Damn him, he was making a habit out of it. She'd thought she was entirely much too tense to be able to relax, even in a hot bubble bath.

She was wrong.

While it didn't erase any of the problems facing her, she did feel some of the tension leeching from her body. With a contented sigh, she slid farther down into the tub and watched the diminishing soap bubbles slowly thin out along the surface of the water. Watching buoyed her spirits.

Things had a way of working themselves out. Wasn't that what she'd always tried to believe? No matter what it took, she'd find a way of keeping custody of the twins. There had to be some rights she could tap into as the technical birth mother, not to mention that having her retain custody of the twins had been Holly's dying wish.

As for her father's condition, well, maybe the diagnosis wasn't as bleak as it sounded. Medical science was progressing by leaps and bounds every day. Maybe a cure, or at least a way to send the disease into remission, could be found. And who knew, having the disease might even make her father more humble.

Or humble, period, she amended, since being "more" humble meant that at one point in his life, he'd had to have been humble in some manner, shape or form. The man had never been humble a day in his life. It wasn't in his nature. Carlton Yarbourough was a conqueror, not a submitter.

He'd find a way to conquer this, too, she thought, attempting to unearth a shaft of confidence.

The water was becoming tepid. Sitting up took more effort than she'd thought. With a sigh, she turned the faucet to the left. A wide stream of hot water started pouring into the tub.

Clusters of bubbles began to form where they made contact with the water that was already there. Steam filled the air, growing thicker.

She closed her eyes again and willed her mind not to do anything but drift.

The trouble with rudderless drifting was that her thoughts slowly began to shift toward Sebastian.

He was being everything she'd ever wanted and

needed him to be. Strong, supportive and just asser-
tive enough to cut through her brash bravado. She
knew she had a tendency to be defensive and com-
bative when her back was to the wall. Life with her
father had done that. There would have been no way
she would have survived her adolescence if she
hadn't stood up for herself. It was Sebastian who had
reminded her that she was something more than just
a ball of angry feelings. Something softer. That she
was someone who needed to be held and loved. Who
could be held and loved. He had kindled all these
emotions within her and made her feel…

He'd made her feel. It was best if she just left it
at that.

Her eyes began to drift closed again and she gave
herself up to the restful, sensuous feelings that were
slipping over her more and more completely.

The knock on the door penetrated the haze forming around her and she realized that she'd been very
close to falling asleep. Blinking her eyes, she
scrubbed her hands over her face.

"Yes?"

Sebastian's voice came to her through the door.
"Are you all right in there?"

"I'm fine in here." She'd lost track of time. Stephanie reached for a towel and quickly started drying
herself off. "Why?"

He could hear her moving in the bathtub, hear her
rising. He tried not to dwell on the images that created in his mind.

"I was beginning to worry. You don't usually listen to what I tell you to do and you've been in there a long time."

Discarding the towel, she reached for her robe. "I guess it's time to come out."

He hadn't meant to rush her. "Stay if you like. Are you pruney yet?"

"Why don't you come in and see?"

The instant the words were out of her mouth, she had no idea what had prompted her to say them. Maybe it was soaking in the tub for so long. The water had somehow lowered her resistance so that she said what was really on her mind.

Sebastian reached for the doorknob, then dropped his hand to his side. No sense in putting himself in the path of temptation. "I'll take your word for it."

The sound of her own laughter surprised her. It felt good to laugh. "Chicken."

"If I have to be a fowl, I'd rather think of myself as an owl."

"An owl?" She definitely couldn't envision him as an owl.

"Wise."

To his surprise, the bathroom door opened. "Owls have huge eyes and square bodies. Your eyes are pretty near perfect and your body..." Her voice trailed off.

She was wearing a thin cotton robe that adhered to her still damp body in places like a second skin.

That same old gut-tightening feeling throbbed through him. He fought hard to shut it out.

"What about my body?"

She raised her face, bringing it closer to his. "*Square* is not the word for it."

Right about now, he figured *needy* was the word for it. He was struggling not to take her into his arms. Hell, he was struggling not to pull that flimsy thing right off of her.

"Stevi, maybe you'd better get dressed."

There was desire in his eyes, desire that made her feel beautiful. It had been a long time since she'd felt beautiful. "Why?"

He allowed himself one small touch. Just of her face. He framed one cheek with his thumb and forefinger stretched out along the outline. Damn, but he did want her. "Because I'm only human."

"Go on." The whispered words hovered warmly along his face. Her eyes encouraged him.

His mouth felt suddenly dry. As if cotton wads had been stuffed into it.

"That's just it, if you don't get dressed, I will go on." *I'll make love to you, Stephanie, and then we'll both be damned.* "And I don't think you'd want me to do that."

The smile on her lips began in her eyes and drew him in. "See, you're not always right about everything, either."

She was dancing on dangerous ground and he could warn her only so much. "Stevi—"

The ache inside of her grew. She wanted him to hold her. If he couldn't love her, he could at least pretend for a little while that he did. She thought of the child she'd lost. The one he didn't know about. A sadness filled her.

"Those babies should have been yours," she murmured. "I should have been yours."

The light from the fixtures just behind her caught the shimmer of tears in her eyes. Blended with the sensuality of the moment, it was an incredible one-two combination punch that had him really floored and all but shattered his resistance.

He didn't know how much longer he could continue keeping her at bay for her own good. Because it certainly wasn't for his.

"Stevi, don't—"

Something painful scraped against her soul. He didn't want her. Even for a night. "Don't what? Throw myself at you? Don't worry, you don't have to catch me. You should have gotten good at that, at not catching me. You've had enough practice—"

What control he was trying to exercise snapped. Grasping the lapels of her robe, he dragged her to him and sealed his lips to hers. With fire coursing through his veins, reaching all parts of him, Sebastian kissed her over and over again, holding her to him, molding her body to his.

He wanted her. Wanted Stephanie so badly he couldn't even breathe. Kissing her only brought all of that home to him.

But he'd remained here to do a good deed, not to satisfy any demands clawing inside of him, trying to tunnel out. He had to remember that. Focus on that.

Sebastian drew his head back. She looked dazed when she looked up at him, confusion in her eyes. There was something so enticingly innocent about her, despite the children she'd borne. He felt his desire only growing stronger.

"Last chance," he warned her, praying she would retreat. Because he couldn't.

Stephanie's eyes met his. Her arms remained where they were, entwined around his neck. "To bail out or go forward?"

"Bail out." The hoarse words scraped against his throat.

She ran the tip of her tongue along her lips to moisten them. "What makes you think I want to?"

"Stevi—"

She rose up on her toes again. "Shut up and kiss me again. Damn, but I don't remember you being this talkative before." Her body touching his, she tightened her arms around his neck. "I need you, Sebastian. Right now, I really, really need you. Please don't make me beg."

As if she'd ever needed to. He placed his finger gently across her lips to silence her.

"You don't have to beg, Stevi," he told her softly. "I just don't want you to do something in the heat of the moment."

But that was just the point. "Don't you understand? I *need* the heat of the moment. I need to be reduced just to a mass of nothing more than responses and sensations.'' Her sigh was weary as it touched his face. ''I'm tired of thinking, tired of worrying. Make it all go away, Sebastian.'' She tilted her head even more, her mouth hovering near his. ''Make it all go away.''

A man of stone would have given in to her, Sebastian thought, and he was far from that. He was only flesh and blood and a tangled mass of needs that were threatening to overwhelm him.

''I'll do my best,'' he promised, as he lowered his mouth to hers and silently prayed that she wouldn't regret this too much come the morning.

Because no matter what the outcome, there was no question in Sebastian's mind that he never would.

Chapter Ten

Very slowly, as his lips slanted over hers again and again, desire flowering and growing, Sebastian slipped his hand beneath her robe. Ever so gently, his fingers caressed her still dampened skin.

Stephanie's breath caught in her throat as her body ignited.

She'd been a young girl the last time Sebastian had touched her like this, not the independent woman, with a web design business of her own and babies depending on her, that she was now.

But all the years from there to here vanished in a heartbeat as she felt his hand glide along her body, felt him urgently possess her.

She was twenty again. And completely his.

Her heart pounding madly, Stephanie felt like a brightly lit Roman candle, ready to go off and shower light into the night. An eagerness took hold of her, making her want to feel the stars exploding within her. Making her want to reach journey's end both quickly and languidly.

She couldn't have it both ways.

She wanted it, anyway. To savor the delicious sensations running through her body. To absorb that culminating moment when the final rush came.

Like a separate entity, divorced from any control she could exercise over it, Stephanie's body trembled with each sweep of his hand, with every tantalizing, slow caress. The very core of her quickened in memory. In anticipation.

Just as she'd asked him to do, he stole her thoughts from her, sending them spinning away as passions and needs consumed her.

A moan escaped her lips as Stephanie sank deeper into his kiss.

This was wrong, he knew it was wrong. He shouldn't be allowing this to happen because nothing had changed between them.

Nothing and everything.

The reasons he'd left were still there, still a barrier between them. Added to that, they'd lived seven years' worth of long days and longer nights without each other. Forged lives that were emotionally and physically hundreds of miles away from where they had once been. She wasn't the fiery, petulant girl he'd lost his heart to almost from first sight. And he wasn't the poor boy with a single pair of shoes. They were completely different people now.

And yet...

And yet the taste of her mouth, the scent of her skin, the way laughter bubbled up in her throat, that hadn't changed. His need to have her hadn't changed, either. Or, if it had, it had only intensified. Any lies he'd told himself over the years to the contrary were just that. Lies. He'd never gotten over Stephanie, though God knew he had tried. Tried to bury his need for her in hot, steamy nights spent with other women whose names he didn't recall, whose faces he couldn't remember.

They couldn't replace her, couldn't erase her.

No one had ever mattered, no one but Stephanie.

As she pressed her body against his insistently, Sebastian could feel his own begin to burn from wanting her. His breath quickening in his lungs, he grasped the sash at her waist and dissolved the knot beneath his fingers.

Then, very slowly, to tease himself as well as Stephanie, Sebastian parted her robe, slipping it from her shoulders by inches.

It slid to the floor like a sigh.

The sigh mingled with her sharp intake of breath as he touched her. Worshipfully, his hands passed over her as he rememorized every curve, every inch, dragging away the cobwebs from his mind.

He remembered every moment of the last time, the

only time, they'd made love. It made his desire all that more zealous in its demands upon his body.

He wanted to tell her that he was sorry, that he couldn't help himself, because somehow, he'd crossed some imaginary line without fully realizing it and now there was no turning back. But there were no words. Every shred of energy was devoted to this moment, to loving her. The way he always had.

The way he always would.

She'd dreamed about this. Locked away in the chambers of her mind, coaxed out only in the darkness of night and under the guise of dreams, was an intense desire that had her living for this moment: to have him want her. To have him take her again, the way he once had.

There wasn't even the tiniest part of her that wasn't on fire.

Eagerly, Stephanie began to pull him free of his clothing, desperately wanting to touch his body, to feel him against her, his skin touching hers. She ripped the last button off his shirt as she tried to yank his shirt off his shoulders.

The button pinged as it landed on the tile floor behind her.

"Damn," she muttered under her breath, her fingers tangling in her eagerness.

He laughed, the sound echoing against her lips. "It was loose, anyway."

Loose. Like all her inhibitions, she thought. They'd all been set loose, to flee while their space became filled in with a desire so intense, it hardly allowed her to draw in a breath.

Her pulse beat double time as she unfastened his belt, then sent his jeans to the floor.

Somehow, they'd gotten to her bed, though she wasn't sure just how, and Sebastian's long, lean torso was as devoid as hers of any covering. A trail of his clothing littered the floor from the bathroom to the bed, a testimony to the urgency that vibrated within her body and his.

Lost in an embrace, they sank onto her bed, one kiss flowering into another, each echoing a promise of what was to come.

With each touch of his hand, she felt her body growing more and more tense with anticipation, riper for the moment when he would take her.

She didn't know if she could stand the wait, no matter how small. It had been so long, so very long since he had loved her.

There'd been no other lovers, none but him no matter how much she'd tried to care about someone else, and her body was beyond being ready to be taken again.

He wanted to stop. Heaven knew the same so-called noble thoughts that had kept him from her side all these years, that had taken him away to begin with, were still there within him, echoing protests. But they were just tiny flickers on the head of a match while this inferno of desire was consuming him, claiming every inch of him, refusing to abate or loosen its grip.

Over and over again Sebastian kissed her, anointing every part of her body with deep, moist, open-mouthed kisses that had her quivering, growing damper still as she arched against him, trying to absorb every tiny movement, every available scrap.

"If you don't take me soon, I'm going to have to attack you," she whispered hoarsely as a climax teased the outer perimeter of her soul. Just as his fingers teased at the wanting center of her core.

Unable to focus, Stephanie reached for him blindly, her hands touching air.

"No need," he answered, his voice just as hoarse as hers from wanting her, from the restraint that was almost breaking free of his rein.

He wanted to pleasure her, to bring her up to the very summit of ecstasy before he took her. Because there might never be a second time. His control, he promised himself, would be better once this was over, once he had her this one last time.

But right now, the needs Sebastian felt holding him prisoner were so huge, he hadn't a prayer of standing in their way.

With his eyes on hers, loving her so hard it hurt his heart, Sebastian poised himself over her. She opened her eyes and looked up at him. The look of pure surrender mingled with desire undid him.

With a surrendering groan, he linked his fingers through hers and he slid into her.

The cry she uttered was swallowed up by his lips as he sealed them over hers.

Together, their bodies rocked and began to move in unison, moving faster and faster as the promise beckoned and increased.

The rush that overtook them was all-encompassing, breathtaking and magnificent. Stephanie bit her lip hard to keep from crying out, afraid of waking the babies. Afraid somehow that if the cry left her body, so would part of the euphoric ecstasy that had come over her.

It kept building and building, one wave of excruciating pleasure into another, holding her hard, catapulting her to the next level.

Her mind spun as she dug her fingernails into Sebastian's back, hardly aware of what she was doing. A scream gurgled in her throat, begging to be set free.

And then it was over.

Exhaustion blanketed her as she became aware of things: Her own body sinking into the mattress, the sweet weight of his over hers. And paradise. A paradise populated with flowers and sunshine and so many beautiful things.

Even as she reached for them, they started to fade away.

But she knew that for one shining instant, they had been real. It was enough. And so much more than she'd had.

Sighing, she wrapped her arms around Sebastian

and murmured, "Welcome home," against his cheek.

Guilt skewered him with a double-edged broadsword, drawing blood. Arousing his dormant conscience. He raised his head.

"Stevi—"

She saw the look in his eyes through a haze and refused to allow it to penetrate the thinning shreds of euphoria she still dragged to her.

"If that's an apology hovering on your lips, Sebastian, swallow it." It was neither an entreaty nor an order, just a request. "I don't want you to ruin this moment with any regrets."

Pivoting on his elbows, he framed her face with his hands. How had he managed to live so long, away from those eyes, away from that smile?

"The only regret I have, Stevi, is that I can't be who I need to be for you."

She felt tears forming and struggled to keep them from emerging.

"You are," she whispered, not trusting her voice not to break if she spoke any louder. "Don't you understand that? You are. You always were."

Heaven help him, but she knew just how to undo him, how to undo all his noble thoughts and silent promises to himself and to her. For just a moment, he pretended to believe her. Because he wanted to.

Spent, he found himself wanting her all over again. Gathering her in his arms, he looked down into her face. A hell of a doctor he was. She'd given birth just more than three weeks ago, and even though he knew that many women were fit to have relations as soon as two weeks after the event, Stephanie hadn't been checked over by her doctor.

He'd allowed his own desire to overrule his common sense, his profession, everything.

Concern etched a place for itself beside his guilt, and even though it was too late to ask, he did, anyway. "I didn't hurt you, did I?"

Making love with him had felt nothing short of wondrous. She touched her lips quickly to his. "The only way you could have done that was to turn away from me again."

But he should have, he thought. He should have. "Stevi—" he began, but she silenced him, her finger to his lips.

"Shh. No words. Actions speak so much louder." Her eyes on his, she moved her body in slow circles. She got the response she was after. A smile teased her lips as a glint of mischief entered her eyes. A glint he hadn't seen in seven years. "And unless I'm mistaken, I have the distinct impression you're about to go into action again."

He laughed, feeling himself hardening within her. "I never could hide anything from you."

Only your heart, Sebastian, she thought. *Only your heart.*

But in the next moment, there was no more room for thoughts. Only feelings, and she gave herself up to them gladly. If she had only tonight, then so be it. But she intended to enjoy every tiny scrap of that night to its fullest extent.

As he held her in the wee hours of the morning, while the rest of the world slept, they'd talked a little, tilting carefully with words, afraid of losing the small happiness they'd uncovered. Sebastian had offered to accompany her to her father's house, knowing she needed to go to him. To have things out in the open.

"You don't have to go alone. I can go with you."

Much as she wanted to have him there, she knew the danger of relying on someone other than herself. If she leaned on him, she'd only fall hard when he moved aside. She shook her head. "It's better that I have it out with him on a one-on-one basis."

He understood. This was her fight and she needed to undertake at least this phase of it alone. He tightened his arm around her.

"Have it your way, slugger."

So in the morning he'd left to check in on his mother and change before he went to the office, and she had waited for Iris to arrive at the house before girding herself up for what lay ahead.

The drive to her father's house seemed to take longer than the miles would have warranted. Nerves rode in the passenger seat, accompanying her. Growing larger with each mile that passed.

Her hands felt damp holding on to the steering wheel. Even when she stood up to him, her father could always do that to her. Unhinge her confidence.

It was something he did to everyone. A knack he heavily counted on to serve him in the courtroom. He was a vanquisher, a spoiler, and he took no prisoners. Even with his own children.

It had been several years since she'd even entered her father's house. Several years since she had stormed out, slamming the door behind her and closing a chapter of her life she had never intended to revisit.

But time, she thought as she approached the long winding road that would bring her up to her father's house, had a way of changing things. The two words she now realized weren't real were *never* and *forever*.

Because here she was, she thought, pulling up the hand brake on her car and parking in the driveway, facing *never*.

Taking a deep breath, she stepped out of the vehicle and closed its door. It was nine o'clock, but she knew she would find her father still in. She knew his routine. Her father never left for the office until after ten. Anything earlier was not a decent hour to him. He left it to his junior partners and law clerks to handle all the details that sprang up within the office, both before he arrived and after.

Like one to the manor born, he only turned his attention to the most important matters, eschewing the mundane and the trivial. That was for lesser lawyers, lawyers who were not of Carlton Yarbourough's magnitude or reputation.

The housekeeper, a woman in her sixties, looked

a little uncertain as she opened the door to her after Stephanie had given her her name. "If you'll just wait here, I'll tell the judge you're here."

Five years earlier her father had served one term as a judge of the lower appellate court before he felt it bored him to be on that side of the bench, but the title had remained with him. It suited his vanity to hear others address him by it.

"Don't bother," Stephanie told her, already walking down the corridor. "I'll tell him myself."

Predictably, she found her father in his study, a cup of coffee in his hand as he looked out his window at the ocean beyond. She'd once overheard him saying it helped center him. She'd always thought it helped make him feel more godlike, looking down on the sea.

He was in the gray leather wing chair he'd taken from his father's house when her grandfather had died. As she knew he would be.

"You're late, Matthew," he snapped without bothering to look in the direction of the closing door. "You know how I value punctuality."

Well, if his voice was any indication, he certainly sounded healthy enough, she thought. The man always could cut people off at the knees at thirty paces. And she and Matthew were among his favorite targets.

Stephanie took several steps into the room, her eyes never shifting from the back of his head. "You always did value principles a great deal more than you did people, Father.''

Carlton's head snapped up, his eyes darting to the reflection in the window. It took him a moment to mask his surprise before he turned around. But the same reflection that allowed him to see her allowed her to see him.

Stephanie didn't think she'd ever seen her father appear surprised before. A semi-smile curving her lips, she congratulated herself for managing the impossible.

Setting the near empty cup down hard on the desk, Yarbourough glared at her, suspicion etched in his lean face. ''What are you doing here? Where's Matthew?''

He did look older, she thought. Older than she remembered. Older than he should.

''Probably on his way. There's a lot of traffic on the Pacific Coast Highway,'' she told him, referring to the road her brother had to take from his own home. She'd heard the news report just before she'd pulled up in the driveway.

Her father looked pained and inconvenienced at the delay. Matthew served as his chauffeur. Her father hadn't driven a car in more than twenty years. ''If this is about those brats of yours—''

The dismissive, annoyed tone nearly succeeded in putting her off, but she knew that at least this one time, her father had an excuse for the bitter edge in his voice. Life had dealt him a hand he couldn't win against, couldn't find a loophole to, at least not today, and that left him angry and incensed.

"No, this is about you." She saw suspicion flare in his eyes. *Not this time, Father. I'm not afraid of you anymore. You've done your worst and I'm not afraid.* "Why didn't you let me know?"

"Know what?" The voice was guarded, cagey. She wasn't his daughter. She was an adversary he was facing across a courtroom.

She hadn't come here to be intimidated by his look. It was gratifying to know that he didn't have the power over her he'd once had. But he was her father and there was some part of her that cared, even when she told herself that Carlton Yarbourough would probably call her a fool for feeling that way.

Stephanie crossed to his desk. She splayed her hands on the smoothly polished top, leaning over so that her face was close to his.

"Don't play games with me, Father, I'm not some first-year lawyer you have trembling in his shoes. Why didn't you tell me you were ill?"

His eyes grew cold. "I don't know what you're talking about."

She straightened, shaking her head. "I never thought lying became you, even though you're usually so much better at it than now." Her eyes narrowed as she looked at him, refusing to back away. "I know, Father."

He rose. Stephanie noticed that he leaned heavily on the arms of his chair before he gained his feet.

"Damn him, I knew Matthew was too weak to keep this to himself. I should have never given him credit—"

As if her father had ever given anyone credit for anything. Part of her told her she should just turn around and go home. But she remained, stubborn as the man she was confronting.

"Don't blame Matthew, I found out by accident. And he wouldn't have been weak to tell me," she insisted angrily, losing her temper despite herself. "No more than you would have been."

"Don't preach at me, young woman. It's my health and I choose who knows and who doesn't. And I choose to say that it's none of your business if I have some sort of condition or not." He stood only a few inches taller than she did. "You're not supposed to know."

"Why? Why aren't I supposed to know, Father? Because it would make me think you were human?" She laughed shortly, angry at the man who had robbed her of so many things, like affection. Like a happy childhood to look back upon. "Guess what, I already think that."

"I don't care what you think," he shouted. "I don't want you or anyone else knowing because it makes me seem vulnerable—"

He did think he was some sort of god, she thought in disgust. "You're that, too, Father. Damn it, we all are. Don't you understand that?"

"No," he said fiercely. "Not me. Maybe you, maybe your brother, but not me."

Chapter Eleven

Stephanie looked at her father for a long moment in silence.

"So you're invincible, is that it?" Her father drew back his shoulders. Just the way she did, she realized. But his looked so thin now. Had they always been that way and she just hadn't noticed?

His eyes all but bore into hers. "Damn straight I am."

Just like old times, his arrogance grated on her. Why was she bothering? Life-threatening illness or not, there was just no changing the man.

"You go on believing that, Father. Maybe you can even convince yourself of it after a while." She re-thought her words. "Hell, you probably *have* con-

vinced yourself already. Me—'' she shrugged
''—I'm just mortal. I figure everyone needs someone
in their lives to be there for them. To care if something happens.''

''And you care?'' The words dripped with sarcasm. ''You care that I have bone cancer?''

Bone cancer. The diagnosis slashed through her
like a high-powered buzz saw.

But she knew the last thing her father wanted was
to see pity in her eyes. Gathering herself together,
she met his numbing glare head-on and raised her
chin, refusing to be cowed by this man the way she
knew so many others were. ''Yes, I care. Maybe that
makes me stupid in your book, but I care.''

It wasn't good enough. He was accustomed to
tearing statements apart, to getting down to the underbelly, the very core. ''Why?''

He would ask that, she thought. It was so like him.
He just couldn't believe, couldn't take anything at
face value, even the truth.

She shrugged again, a careless lifting of her shoulders. ''Damned if I know. Because you're my father.'' Her voice softened just an iota. ''Because
everyone deserves to have someone worry about
them, even if just a little.'' She looked into his eyes.
''Even you.''

He blew out a breath, whether in contempt or pure
mystification, she didn't know. ''You never were
very bright, were you?''

Her eyes narrowed. She wasn't going to take the

bait. Wasn't about to yell or retreat, which was what she knew he wanted, to goad her. To make her leave. Even after all this time, she could still second-guess her father. She tossed her head. "Bright enough to get out from under your thumb."

He surprised her then by laughing. The effort seemed to weaken him. Like a balloon losing air, he sank onto his chair, but he continued to laugh. For the first time, he looked at her with something that seemed akin to respect, she realized.

Or maybe it was just a trick played by the sunlight streaming into the room.

"You should have been my son."

When she was very young, she'd felt guilty that she couldn't be what he'd so obviously wanted her to be. A male child. Someone to carry on his work and his name. But that was a long time ago. She knew now that there was nothing to be guilty about.

"I should have been exactly what I am. What's inside doesn't depend on gender, Father, it never has." Grappling with her patience, Stephanie looked at him. She wanted to hear this from him, not secondhand, not from Matthew, but from him. "Now, what did the doctor tell you?"

Carlton waved a thin, fine-boned hand at the question and the notion of the specialist he'd visited. "The man is a quack."

They both knew better than that. "If he was a quack, you wouldn't be going to him. You've never had any patience with incompetence on any level. Now, what is he telling you?''

Yarbourough turned the chair away from her. ''Nothing I wanted to hear.''

That she could readily believe. Whatever this was, it had to be bad. ''Are you getting treatment?''

He wasn't about to have her prying into his affairs. ''That doesn't concern you.''

She straightened. There was just so far her good intentions would take her and no further. It wasn't as if she didn't have problems of her own. Her father had been shutting her out all of her life. Why in heaven's name had she expected him to change now just because she was ready to forgive him?

She clamped down on her emotions. ''Right, I forgot. You're a god and I'm a mortal.'' She moved closer to the door. There really wasn't anything left to say. ''Well, if you decide that you need a mortal to talk to, you know my number.'' And then she paused, rethinking the last sentence. ''No, you probably don't, do you. But Matthew does. Talk to him.''

She was almost at the door when she heard her father clear his throat. Her back to him, she waited for a beat. And then he spoke. ''Matthew says you're keeping the twins.''

Stephanie turned around slowly. She knew how vehemently he'd disapproved of her being a surrogate mother. Almost as much as he had disapproved of Sebastian. ''Yes, I am.''

Yarbourough had never cared that much for children—especially not the everyday care and feeding of them. Her reasons for being a surrogate mother completely eluded him. "Why?"

She shook her head. "You wouldn't understand."

But that was the easy way out and maybe that was what was wrong. Explaining was harder, but he needed to hear it, at least once and from her. Needed to hear how he had branded her.

Her eyes narrowed as she looked at her father. "Because I have all this excess love I never got to spend anywhere. Mother left, you were never there to begin with, Matthew was too busy with his friends and you chased off Sebastian." A smile played on her lips as she thought of the infants. Even now they were taking on personalities of their own. Holly fussed while Brett seemed like the epitome of a happy baby. She wanted to be there, in their lives, to see how they turned out. "At least with the twins, I get to begin fresh. They need me. That's something I know you don't understand, Father. Human need. But they do, they need me and I need them. Besides, I love them."

She turned her back on him, afraid that he'd see just how much he'd managed to hurt her, how much she had once wanted his respect, his approval. More than that, his love.

How much, in a way she supposed, she still did.

"Stephanie."

Her hand on the doorknob, she told herself to just keep going, that her father probably only had something disparaging to say. That was his way, cutting people down to tiny nubs.

But she turned around, anyway, calling herself a hopeless fool. Or maybe a hopeful one.

His own mortality was eating away at him, weakening him more than the disease he was suffering ever could. He didn't believe in leaving loose ends for the last minute. He never had, and maybe this needed to be said. A man needed a clear conscience when he died, and Yarbourough knew he hadn't lived an exemplary life, not in some aspects. "I'm sorry."

Stephanie stared at her father in dumbfounded silence. She would have bet anything that the simple words were not in his repertoire. He looked as if they had burned his tongue on their way out.

As the surprise of their emergence subsided, Stephanie could appreciate just how difficult it was for him to say them.

"I know," she responded quietly. Then added, "Me, too."

Knowing that anything further couldn't be hoped for today, she walked out.

Stephanie let out the breath she was holding. Though she'd come regularly to Sheila for her checkups over the last nine months, she'd never managed to relax during an exam. Exam mercifully over, she scooted back up on the table. "Thanks for fitting me in today."

Sheila flashed a quick smile. "No problem. I had a last-minute cancellation. Things worked out well for both of us." Sheila pushed away on the small stool, stripping the latex gloves from her hands. She tossed them into the wastebasket before looking at Stephanie. "You've had relations."

Slightly embarrassed even though she knew there was no reason to be, Stephanie sat up. "Can't hide anything from you, can I?"

"Not that sort of thing, no. Not when you did it within the last twenty-four hours." Getting off the stool, she made a few notations in Stephanie's file. When she looked up, her smile was warm, understanding. "Was that why you canceled your appointment?"

"No." Stephanie slid off the table and began to hurry into the clothes she'd left draped over the arm of the chair in the corner. "I guess I was just overwrought."

"Small wonder, seeing what you have to deal with." Sheila closed the file and then held it against her. "Want to talk? I have a few minutes to spare."

Her first instinct was to say no, but that would be too much like her father. She said the only thing she felt she could honestly share. "The twins' grandmother wants me to hand over custody to her."

Sheila leaned a hip against the side counter, waiting. "And?"

Stephanie closed the buttons on her dress and

stepped into her shoes. "I don't want to give them up."

Sheila had been the doctor she had turned to for the implanting of Holly's embryos into her womb. And the woman knew the heartache she'd gone through when she'd heard of the accident. Rather than any of her friends or Matthew, Sheila had been the first one she'd turned to.

The woman placed an arm around her shoulder now and gave her a small squeeze. "Possession being nine-tenths of the law notwithstanding, you're going to need a good lawyer."

Stephanie picked up her purse, nodding grimly. "Yes, I know."

Sheila hesitated for a moment, debating. "Your father—"

Stephanie cut her off before she could get any further. "—doesn't think I should keep the twins, either. Thanks, but I'll manage."

It wasn't like Stephanie to be abrupt. Sheila figured the other woman was having a very difficult time of it and hoped that didn't cause her to make mistakes blindly.

"You know," Sheila said philosophically, her tone gentle, kind, "in a storm, oaks can break. Willows survive because they can bend." She patted her on the arm before opening the door and stepping out of the room. "Don't be afraid to lean on someone."

Wasn't that what she'd just said to her father?

Stephanie's short laugh was self-deprecating. "Thanks, I'll try to remember that."

Sheila paused for one more moment to lean into the room, lowering her voice in confidence. "And the next time you give birth remember to come and see your doctor before you start 'entertaining.' Lucky for you you're as strong as a horse. Some women have to wait a good six weeks before having relations again. I hope you found someone who deserves you."

Stephanie only shrugged noncommittally, saying nothing. She couldn't help wondering what her doctor would have to say if Sheila knew that it was her new partner she'd slept with.

Her mouth curved in memory. Not that much sleeping had gone on.

She had to be getting back. What with her visit to her father and then her appointment, she'd left Iris alone with the babies too long. Checking her purse for her charge card, Stephanie hurried out of the room. And straight into Sebastian.

He caught her by the arms before he fully realized it was her. Surprised, he continued to hold her as he asked, "What are you doing here?"

"Making up for the checkup I neglected." She glanced at his hands and he dropped them belatedly. "Doctor says I'm terrific."

He smiled and lowered his voice, glancing to see if either one of the two nurses at the desk was listening. They didn't appear to be. "I could have told her that. How did your meeting with your father go?''

She shrugged. It would be overly optimistic of her to think they had made a breakthrough. But it had been a minor dent of sorts. ''It went.''

He couldn't read her expression and decided that the old man had probably steamrollered right over her. He banked down his anger. ''Want to talk about it? I could come by later after-hours.''

''No, I don't want to talk about it.'' And she didn't, not yet. ''But you can come by after-hours if you like,'' she added with a smile. ''The twins are getting accustomed to seeing you.''

There were times when she was hard to read. Did their spending the night together make things better or worse? Despite his resolutions to the contrary, he knew exactly which side he wanted to vote for. ''How about the twins' mother?''

The twins' mother. It was the first time anyone had referred to her that way. The words shimmered before her for a second. She was a mother. Their mother. It felt good.

''The jury's still out about that,'' she finally answered, but her smile was inviting. He took it to be a good sign. ''Come by and make your case. Last night was a good opening argument.''

He laughed. ''You were the one in charge of arguing. I was handling negotiations.''

A broad grin slid over her lips. ''Is that what you call it?''

If they weren't in the middle of his office, he would have kissed her right here and now. Instead, he contented himself with just looking at her. Almost devoid of makeup, her hair pulled back in a ponytail that made her look almost like a teenager instead of the twenty-seven-year-old mother of twins, she was still the loveliest creature he had ever seen.

"That's what I call it."

"Then maybe we can get down to some more negotiations later," she speculated, her eyes dancing.

"Doctor—" Lisa cleared her throat before raising her voice "—your next patient is waiting," she informed him cheerfully, pointing to the far end of the hall. "That's the coldest room. If you don't get to her soon, she might turn into one giant goose bump."

"Right." Sebastian was already walking down the hall toward the room. "I'll see you later," he promised Stephanie.

If the woman was getting goose bumps, Stephanie speculated as she handed Lisa her charge card to take care of the co-payment minimum on her visit, it wasn't because of the temperature in the examination room. Sebastian was the kind of doctor mothers dreamed about for their daughters. The kind women dreamed about, period.

Taking back her card, Stephanie nodded at Lisa and left the office.

She had more important things on her mind than that, Stephanie told herself as she got into her car five stories down. She needed help and she needed it fast, before Brett's mother escalated the custody fight and made it dirty.

Arriving home twenty minutes later, she paused only long enough to give each baby a warm hug, then went immediately to the phone and called her brother.

"Heard you saw the old man today at the house," he said as soon as she said hello.

Stephanie could hear the admiration in his voice. Though he was older, Matthew tended to shy away from having any words with his father that didn't involve absolute agreement. Of the two of them, he had always been the peacemaker while she'd been the rebel.

"We had a few words," she acknowledged.

"Yeah, I know. He almost took my head off for letting you know. Said it was his business. I take it you rattled him up pretty well."

"I'm sorry, Matthew. I didn't mean to drag you into it."

"Hey, story of my life. Under all that, he did seem to be affected that you actually came. Maybe the old man's got a heart in there, after all."

She wasn't all that sure about that. "A little late in the game to be finding it."

"Never too late, Stef, never too late." She heard him typing in something on his computer. "What did you call about?"

She filled him in about the pending custody battle

as succinctly as possible, ending with, "I need a lawyer, Matt."

The sound of typing ceased. "I'm not that kind of a lawyer, Stef, you know that." He sounded genuinely sorry. "Though he's into criminal law, this is actually more Father's area. Maybe if I talked to him—"

Why did everyone insist on throwing her in with her father? Matthew of all people should know how hopeless that was.

"As you pointed out, he's a criminal lawyer. He's also ill and he's not exactly keen about my being the 'vessel for a science experiment,'" she reminded him, using the exact words, according to Matthew, her father had when what she'd proposed to do had come to his attention nine months ago. "Three very good reasons not to talk to him."

But Matthew didn't agree. "Ill or not, he's got one hell of a great legal mind, Stef. You know that. Nothing he likes better than a good fight." He knew what she was going to say. "And he doesn't have to believe in the cause, he's said so often enough. He just likes the fight. It invigorates him."

Stephanie blew out a breath. There was no way she was going to go to her father with this. She wasn't about to put herself in the position of asking him for a favor. There were other lawyers. "There's nothing criminal going on here, Matt."

"What do you call Brett's mother trying to separate you from the twins? If that isn't criminal—"

He'd managed to surprise her. "Since when did you think so?"

She heard him laugh softly. "Since I saw the look in your eyes when I tried to talk to you about putting them up for adoption. You love those babies, Stef. I wouldn't want to see you lose them."

That was her whole point in calling him. "Then help me."

Reversing gears, he ceased being her brother and became a lawyer instead. She could hear it in his voice. "Best help I can give you is to put your case in front of Father."

Right, nothing her father would like better than to represent her in this. "That's like handing someone a lead-lined life preserver."

"I don't think so," he insisted patiently. "Let me at least try."

She knew he would whether or not she agreed to it. "Go ahead. It's a waste of time, but do it quickly if you have to, and while you're at it, scout around for me. I need to get a good lawyer quickly and we both know it's not going to be Father."

"I'll get back to you within twenty-four hours," he promised, hanging up.

"Right," she muttered under her breath, hanging up the receiver.

In the meantime, Stephanie thought, she was going to start calling around to see if anyone she knew knew a good lawyer.

* * *

By the time Sebastian came over that night, Stephanie felt drained and as far from being in the best of spirits as Honolulu was from experiencing a snowbound Christmas. Iris had left early to attend a granddaughter's birthday party. The instant she left, both twins had sent up a howl. No sooner had she settled them in than her imagination went completely blank, effectively curtailing her plans on getting a jumpstart on one of her new web design accounts.

To top it all off, no one she called knew of a lawyer to refer her to, other than her own father.

So when the doorbell rang at seven-thirty, she fairly stormed over to it. Throwing open the door, Stephanie held it ajar as she looked at him. As far as she was concerned, she wasn't fit for any sort of company.

"Maybe you shouldn't come in."

"Why?" He looked at her, concerned. "Anything wrong?"

She was too tired to explain and give him the long version. Instead, she opted for a short one. "I feel like biting off someone's head."

Was that all? He nodded, moving past her and entering the house. "Don't worry, your hormones'll level out soon."

She hated being lumped in with everyone else. "It's not hormones," she protested. With a sigh, she closed the door. "It's everything else."

"It always is," he replied absently. "I don't see Iris's station wagon."

Stephanie shrugged, following him into the living room. "She had a party to go to."

Now that he thought of it, he recalled his mother saying she was invited to Iris's granddaughter's party. He'd encouraged her to go. "That's right, I forgot. Hungry?"

Stephanie dragged her hand through her bangs. "I don't know."

Sebastian held up a large white bag with a red dragon logo. The bottom of the bag was already becoming stained. "I brought Chinese."

Stephanie melted a little as the aroma of the food hit her. He'd remembered. Chinese food had always been her favorite when they were together. "I guess I could eat a little."

"Always good to keep up your strength," he agreed. The twins had to be sleeping, he decided. He didn't see or hear either of them.

Stephanie followed him as he went to the kitchen and watched him take down two plates from the cupboard. The ease with which he did struck her. "I never thought I'd see you making yourself at home anywhere."

He didn't want her misunderstanding what he was doing here, though damn if he actually understood it. "There's a difference between making yourself at home and just being familiar with things."

"Maybe you should have been a lawyer," she told him. "Maybe then my father would have liked you better."

Sebastian took out the silverware, plunking it down beside the plates. Then, straddling a chair, he proceeded to take out the white cartons and open them.

"'Better' indicates that he liked me to some extent. We both know that wasn't even remotely true. From the look in his eyes, he would have just as soon seen me dead than talk to me."

"The look in his eyes?" She looked at him sharply. "When did you see my father?"

That had been a slip. He hadn't meant to bring that up. "A long time ago. Have an egg roll."

"Food isn't the answer to everything." But she took one, anyway, suddenly finding that her appetite was alive and well.

He avoided her eyes as he dished out the fried rice. "Try telling that to someone who's starving."

She took the serving from him. "You do have *lawyer* written all over you."

He spared her a look. And a grin. "Just comes from dealing with someone who could argue the ears off a stone statue rather than admit that she was wrong."

"Wrong?" She placed a hand dramatically to her breast. "When was I ever wrong?"

"I rest my case," Sebastian deadpanned.

"Just as long as it isn't on top of the Chinese food," she quipped.

Something within her glowed when he smiled at her like that. And just for a little while, as she ate, she pretended that there was no pending court battle in front of her, no ailing father to worry about and that she and Sebastian belonged together.

What could it hurt?

Chapter Twelve

Throughout the meal, though she tried to ignore them, the questions she'd raised in her own mind continued nagging at her. Particularly one question. By the time Stephanie closed the now-sagging, half-empty cartons and began putting them away in the refrigerator, she couldn't hold the question back any longer. It had haunted her for all these years now.

"I promised myself I'd never ask you this." She turned from the refrigerator and looked at him. Pretending nonchalance didn't work, so Stephanie dove in. She had her father's version, but she needed to hear his. From his own mouth. "Why did you leave me?"

Taking the silverware to the sink, Sebastian spared

her only a fleeting glance. He shrugged. "There's no point in going over that."

"Oh, but there is," she insisted. Now that she'd finally said it out loud, she couldn't back away. It was all or nothing. She moved, putting herself directly in his line of vision. Filling it. "I have to know. Why did you just leave without a word? Why didn't you face me?"

He wasn't going to answer her. She saw that. Stephanie felt anger licking at her.

"Do you realize you broke my heart, or didn't that matter to you?" Her face clouded over like an angry sky filled with dark rain clouds. "Just how much *did* my father pay you to forget about me?"

The question was like a slap across his face. How could she think he'd trade being with her for something like money?

"There isn't that much money in the world."

Her father had said he'd paid him off to leave. Who did she believe? And if it hadn't been money, what *had* made him leave? "Then what did he give you as a down payment?"

It took effort to curb the sudden flash of temper that rose within him. "Nothing. He gave me nothing." Sebastian regained control. "What he did was paint a picture for me of what life would be like for you if you married me." Carlton Yarbourough had been very precise in his wording, in his facts. "And he was right. I had nothing to give you. You would have regretted marrying me in six months. Less."

Sebastian paused, then shook his head. "I couldn't stand that."

"Nothing to give me?" Her eyes widened in disbelief. "Nothing to give me?" She felt insulted, incensed. "Did you think that little of me that you thought I had to be bought, that I needed 'things'?" It was a struggle to keep her voice even. "All my life, I've had 'things.'" And none of them mattered. They'd never made her happy. "What I didn't have was someone who loved me. Someone who cared about me." She thought of her father and her mouth turned bitter. "Not how I reflected on them, but me, for myself. Cared about what my feelings were. If something hurt. That's what you 'gave' me. That was worth the world to me."

And he didn't understand that, Stephanie thought, looking at him. Maybe she'd been wrong about Sebastian, after all.

He debated just leaving, without explaining. But maybe she deserved to know. Too much time had passed in the dark for both of them. "Your father came to me the day before we were supposed to run off together. He told me that the kindest thing I could do for you was to leave town—and you. He said that you were headstrong and determined to marry me despite everything he'd pointed out, so he was coming to me, to appeal to my sense of logic and honor." He laughed shortly, sticking his hands deep into his pockets. Like the excellent lawyer he was, Yarbourough had known his audience and just how to play him. "He pointed out how I couldn't give you what you were accustomed to having, that I would drag you down to my level, and that eventually, you'd grow to resent and maybe even hate me for what you were missing out on."

He blew out a breath, looking out her kitchen window. Dusk was quietly creeping in over her lawn, coaxing night in its wake. "Other than wanting to punch his teeth in, I knew your father was right." He lifted one shoulder in a careless shrug. "Maybe that was why I wanted to punch his teeth in." He looked at Stephanie then. "*Because* he was right."

"And so you left—without even talking to me."

He heard the edge in Stephanie's voice. It made him speak all the more softly. "As your father pointed out, you were a little less than rational on the subject—"

She couldn't believe he was actually saying this to her. Stephanie threw up her hands. "The subject was *my life,* I should have had a say in it. I know *he* never thought that, but *you,* you should have."

She felt betrayed all over again. How could he? How *could* he have done this, have bought the load of garbage her father had pushed? It was all about his not wanting Sebastian, a fatherless child, for his son-in-law, nothing more. Her father had never cared whether or not she had things, all he cared about was the family name and how her actions would reflect on him.

"I thought you would have. Do you know how

many nights I laid awake, trying to figure out what I had done to drive you away?'' she demanded hotly. Agitated, she began to pace around the small kitchen. "Trying to figure out how to find you." She'd gone to his mother, begging her to tell where Sebastian had gone, to no avail. "Your mother was a clam, loyal to the very end, so I hired a private investigator." Her mouth twisted in a self-deprecating smile. "By the time he had tracked you down, my pride had finally kicked in. I decided that if you didn't want me, I didn't want you."

He knew he should just let the words pass, but he couldn't. This much he needed her to know. "I never stopped wanting you."

She shook her head, not believing him. "You never came back. Not until your mother needed you."

He sighed. That had been up for a long, internal debate. "I almost didn't come back then, either." He'd thought of having his mother transported to Seattle instead. Sebastian weighed his words carefully. Stephanie had to understand. "I did it for you."

What a crock. "No you didn't," she contradicted angrily. "You did it to be noble. You did it so that I wouldn't be on your conscience." She stopped pacing and confronted him. "Well, guess what? I am. All those awful days and endless nights when I cried because you weren't there, to hold me and be there for me when I lost the baby, let *that* stay on your conscience."

"Baby?" He stared at her, numb from the knees on up. "What baby?"

"Our baby," she shot back. "I was pregnant when you left me." She held her head high, and her eyes grew cold, distant, hiding the wide river of hurt. "But don't worry, that didn't last long. It was as if I couldn't even keep some small part of you in my life. I lost the baby a month after you disappeared."

A baby. They'd conceived a baby. And it had come and gone without his ever having known it. Sebastian felt too stricken to say anything.

Angry, taking his silence as censure, and feeling completely frustrated because she was unable to change the past and, most likely, the future, she realized she was shouting at him. Stephanie pressed her lips together, afraid of crying. She wasn't going to embarrass herself that way.

"Stevi, I didn't know—"

She didn't want to hear him call her that name. That was for the Sebastian who'd loved her. The Sebastian she'd naively thought she was going to spend the rest of her life with.

"Damn you, Sebastian. Damn you for all the time you stole from me." Turning on her heel, she started to hurry out of the room before she broke down.

He caught her by the wrist before she could get away, pulling her to him. When she looked up at him defiantly, he told her, "I stole it from me, too."

She wanted to scream at him, to accuse him of

lying, because if he had felt that way, if he had cared, he would have returned.

But he had returned, she realized slowly. Sebastian *had* held her in his arms, had made love with her. Moreover, he was here now. Despite his protests, he was here, with her. Because he wanted her.

Maybe she was looking at it all wrong.

And maybe she was wrong now, but she didn't want to think about it any longer. Didn't want to wrap herself up in what hadn't been, or what might not be. She wanted what she could get. And if that meant only now, only this minute, so be it. She'd try to work within the parameters she had.

Stephanie touched his cheek, torn between anger and love. The latter began to tip the scale. "There's such a thing as being too noble, you idiot."

"Maybe." He returned the caress, aching for her. Aching for the years that had been lost. For the girl she'd been and the woman she'd grown to be without him. Aching because he hadn't been there when she'd needed him most. "But he was right you know. I would have dragged you down."

That was his opinion, not hers. She shook her head in response. "Not down. I always thought of you as being above him," she told him softly.

He didn't want to talk anymore. Right, wrong, it didn't matter, not tonight. They were just words, just subjective judgments, and all he knew was that right now, in this space of time, what he wanted was her.

He didn't care if that was wrong, or right, he just knew it was.

Before she could say anything more, Sebastian took her into his arms and kissed her. Hard. Kissed her because there was still a part of him that knew this wouldn't last. That they had both changed too much, had too much happen to them, lived lives apart too long, to recapture the innocent desire that had once been theirs.

But he needed to have her tonight, to hold her and bury his face in her hair, to have her scent mingling with his blood. Needed to make love with her and to her. He molded her body to his.

His kiss left no margin for retreat, no space to reconsider. He brought her blood to an instant boil and she could feel the yearning take hold of her in less than a single heartbeat.

She wanted him. Wanted to be nude beneath his body, wanted to have these urgent feelings addressed, met and placated. These feelings that traveled down to the very core of her.

Feverishly, his mouth slanted against hers over and over again while his fingers worked the long parade of buttons from her throat to her hips free of their confining holes. Exhilarated, anxious, Stephanie dragged his shirt from his body as he slipped his hands behind her back and unhooked her bra.

Stephanie felt everything within her beginning to vibrate in heated anticipation. Her fingers got in one another's way as she undid his belt, then the hook on his trousers. Something quickened within her belly as she pushed the material from his hips. She shivered from the same feeling as he stripped away her underwear.

Within seconds their naked bodies were pressed against each other's, seeking the heat, the solace that could only be found within the other.

He wanted to pleasure her, to make the moments stretch and last, but his own needs hammered against him with an urgency he was powerless to ignore and nearly unable to keep in some semblance of abeyance.

She was as frenzied as he. Whether she was taking her cue from him or felt the same, he didn't know. All Sebastian knew was that she matched him, demand for demand, kiss for kiss. She wanted to possess and be possessed as much as he did.

It nearly sent him over the brink. His tempo increased. He couldn't get enough of her, not the feel, not the taste, not the scent of her.

The bedroom was leagues away, completely unattainable. Locked in an embrace, they slid to the kitchen floor.

Concern moved his ardor aside for a fraction of a moment. His body hovering over hers, he drew back his head. "Am I hurting you?"

It took her a moment to hear him, a moment more to understand that he meant because of the floor. The tiles were hard against her back.

Stephanie's mouth curved. He'd picked a hell of

a time to be thoughtful, just when she felt as if she was going to explode.

"I may never go back to carpet again," she murmured just before she drew his face down to hers and kissed him as hard as he had her.

The next moment, unable to wait, he joined his body to hers and as one, they began to move toward the ultimate pleasure they knew was waiting for them.

He did his best to prolong it, but finally, there was no escaping the final moment. It burst upon them like a shower of stars.

Exhausted, Sebastian slowly sank onto her. He did his best to pivot the weight on his elbows. His perspiration mingled with hers, coating them both.

"Are you all right?" he finally managed to ask, afraid he was crushing her.

"Great," she murmured, gently playing her fingers along his back, feeling so euphoric she could hardly believe that she'd been so totally consumed with angry feelings just a short while ago. "I'm great." Her eyes smiled up into his. "Sure beats the hell out of eating a fortune cookie."

Sebastian laughed. She was referring to the fact that the woman who had taken his order had forgotten to pack fortune cookies for dessert in the take-out bag he'd brought home to her.

"Then I guess you won't mind if I nibble on you," he whispered against her skin, his teeth just lightly grazing her ear.

Stephanie shivered. She could feel it happening again, that wild flash of excitement spiking through her, that desire to be his. It was starting all over.

She laced her arms around his neck. ''Not in the least.''

The telephone's insistent ringing jangled its way into her consciousness as she lay dozing beside Sebastian. His arm was draped protectively around her and she was loathe to leave the warming shelter it created within her.

They'd made love twice more that evening, interrupted once by the twins, who'd gone off in unison, needing to be changed and fed. She'd tried not to think how right it felt, having Sebastian there beside her, caring for Brett as she took care of Holly. Tried not to let his gaze warm her as he watched while she fed each twin in turn.

They'd turned in early once the babies were asleep, to pick up where they'd left off and just to be with each other.

Playing house, she called it in her mind. Stephanie told herself not to become used to it, that all this would change and he would leave her. Again.

But for now, as it was happening, she wanted to enjoy it. Somewhere along the line, after the last time they'd made love, they'd fallen asleep in each other's arms.

The telephone was not a welcome sound. Reaching past him, she groped for the receiver, then drew it to her side of the bed.

Her eyes shut again, she murmured "Hello?" hoping it was a wrong number.

The voice on the other end of the line picked up on her tone. "It's ten o'clock at night. Since when do you fall asleep so early?"

She turned to look at Sebastian, smiling at him. "A new mother's got to get her sleep where she finds it," she quipped. 'Matthew," she mouthed for Sebastian's benefit when he raised a quizzical brow and nodded toward the receiver. "So what are you doing talking in my sleep? What can I do for you?"

"More like what I can do for you," Matthew told her. "I've decided to represent you, Stephanie."

Even half asleep, she could read between the lines. "He turned you down, didn't he? Or rather, me down," she corrected.

The hesitation on the other end was infinitesimal. Had she not been in tune with her brother, she wouldn't have picked up on it. "He said he was too busy to take on another case."

That was an excuse and they both knew it.

"When he was handling the Payton case, he had two others going at the same time," she reminded him, referring to the high-profile case of several years ago. The trial had her father's face visible on the evening news and in every major paper in the country for the length of the run. He'd defended a prominent congressman from criminal charges brought against him. Against all odds, her father had won. He wouldn't have tolerated anything less.

She heard Matthew sigh. It was hard on him, she thought, trying to constantly bring both sides together and receiving nothing but flak, at least from her father. "He's gotten older."

That might have been an excuse for some men, but not for her father. "And no less stubborn. Don't apologize for him, Matthew. I really don't care." All right, maybe she was lying, maybe a tiny part of a tiny part of her did care. But so what? "If you remember, I asked you to be my lawyer, not Father, and I'm very happy you accepted the case."

Unlike their father, Matthew didn't parade his confidence around like some strutting peacock. "Check back with me about that after the case is over."

"Always the optimist." He'd win for her, she thought. He had to. "I'll meet you in your office tomorrow," she promised.

She heard him rustling papers and assumed he was looking through his schedule for the next day. "How's twelve? I can fit you in during lunch."

She knew she could rely on him. "I feel special. Twelve it is." Leaning over her side of the bed, she reached for the pen and paper on the nightstand, which she kept there in case she had any ideas in the middle of the night regarding the accounts she handled. "I'll bring a turkey and ham on rye," she said. It had been Matthew's lunch of choice while he'd been an undergraduate.

"Then I guess I'll have to have Molly let you in," he said, referring to the sixty-five-year-old secretary who was invaluable to him. "See you then."

Leaning over Sebastian to hang up the telephone receiver, she felt her breasts brushing against his chest. She could feel herself beginning to tingle all over again.

Their eyes met as she withdrew to her side of the bed. His expression was mild, but she could see desire flowering in his eyes.

"Matthew taking the case?"

She nodded. "He brought it to my father first—" She tried to check her anger and succeeded for the most part. "I told him not to bother, but he went ahead and asked him, anyway."

"Maybe Matthew thought he could talk your father into it, given his condition." He tucked his arm around her again. "Facing mortality makes you rethink your position on a lot of things."

Stephanie shook her head. She knew better. "Not my father. He's always believed he was right and that God was permanently on his side. You don't rethink from a position like that, you mandate." And her father was good at that, at issuing orders imperiously. Whatever had possessed her to think he might have changed? That he actually *needed* her? Stephanie sighed, her breasts rising and falling beneath the thin sheet that covered her. "We'll be fine."

"Yes, you will." Caught by something in his

voice, Stephanie looked at him. "You're not in this alone," Sebastian told her.

Don't start believing in white knights and promises, she warned herself. *That was only a trap.* "Look who's talking, Houdini."

He had the good grace to wince. Then he trailed his fingers along her face as he smiled. "I'm not going anywhere." At least, not now, not when she needed him. Later, when things were restored to order, when her life was on an even keel again, then he could rethink his position about leaving. But not now.

"Famous last words." She liked the sound of them, but she refused to allow herself to believe. She wasn't about to get hurt again.

"For tonight," he agreed, gathering her to him. "Last words for tonight," he added when she looked at him, confused. "I don't want to talk anymore."

A smile began to play on her lips as she felt his reaction to her growing against her. "Sleepy?"

He cupped her chin with his hand, turning her mouth to his. "Not really."

She batted her eyelashes at him in an exaggerated fashion. "Then I'm out of guesses."

"Good." He rose just a little for leverage, his mouth a breath away from hers. "Because as you pointed out before, actions speak louder than words and I'm in the mood for a little action."

Mischief danced in her eyes. "Just a little?"

"We'll see how the evening goes," he told her, his lips already brushing seductively over hers.

She flicked her tongue over the outline of her lips, tempting him. "Sounds like a plan to me."

"I'm glad you approve."

Sebastian knew she was given to having the last word. His mouth covered hers before she could respond. He felt her words melt against his lips and fade away, unspoken.

His ardor deepened as his kiss did.

Chapter Thirteen

"Taking the afternoon off, this sounds serious." Sebastian looked up from his breakfast to see his mother entering the kitchen. "I couldn't help overhearing you on the telephone with your new boss," she explained.

He'd called Sheila at home when he'd gotten in this morning, explaining the situation. "She understands. As a matter of fact, Stephanie's one of her patients."

He watched his mother crossing the floor slowly, a general determined not to be vanquished by the newest enemy. He supposed that was where he got his own stubborn streak from. From watching his mother battle odds all of her life and win.

"And it's not serious, Ma," he pointed out, correcting her. "I just thought I'd be there for Stephanie."

Geraldine looked at him innocently. "I'm not criticizing—"

He couldn't remember ever hearing his mother criticize anyone. "No, but you are making more of it than you should."

Pouring herself a glass of orange juice, Geraldine paused as she leaned against the counter for balance. "Am I?" She studied him. "Don't forget, I've known you a lot longer than you've known yourself." Putting the carton away, she made her way to the table. "When you went off, supposedly to 'find' yourself seven years ago, I already knew where you were."

Humor lifted the corners of his mouth as he rose with his coffee cup and went to the sink. He liked the whimsical term she used for the years he'd been away. "You could have told me and spared me the trouble."

Trying not to lean too heavily on her cane, Geraldine reached for his plate and took it to the sink in his wake. She shook her head sagely.

"Wouldn't have done any good. Children never listen to their parents. They have to find things out for themselves." She raised her eyes to look at his. "Like who they're destined to spend the rest of their lives with."

Taking the plate from her, he placed it in the sink. "Oh, so now it's destiny?"

"Yes, destiny," she assured her son. "Some people go through their whole lives without meeting their soul mate. Others are fortunate enough to stumble across them sometime during their existence. And a very few have them thrown their way twice in a lifetime." Geraldine's meaning was clear. "Don't miss the pitch."

Folding his arms before him, he leaned back against the sink and looked at his mother. She'd never been one to offer advice if she wasn't asked for it, and he wondered at the change in behavior. "You're talking about Stephanie."

"I'm talking about Stephanie."

Ordinarily, he'd drop the subject, but this was his mother and he wanted to know. "Tell me, I'm curious. How can you say this with any sort of authority, you hardly know her."

"I know enough," she said with confidence. "I know what I saw in her eyes those times she came to the house and to the restaurant, hoping I'd tell her where you were."

It had broken her heart to turn the young woman away. There was no doubt in her mind that Stephanie needed a little "work," but beneath the edginess, there was pure gold. A good match for her son.

He'd wondered about this a great deal. "Why didn't you?"

Because she felt tired, Geraldine drifted back to the table and sat down.

"Don't think I wasn't tempted. But I'd always had faith in your ultimate judgment. I figured if things were meant to be, they would be. If not, then there was a reason for it." Her philosophical bent faded. "But I swear, boy, if you pass this up again, I might not be responsible for my reaction this time."

Having a few minutes before he had to leave, he joined her at the table. There was something almost heartwarming about seeing his mother riled up. "Oh, and what makes this time different?"

"I'd like to see grandchildren before my time on earth is up." She touched his cheek fondly, remembering what he'd been like as a boy. She'd taken hundreds of photographs of him while he'd been growing up, and every so often, she'd sit down with the albums she'd painstakingly organized in date order and just flip through them, reliving the past. "You're the best part of me, Sebastian, and I suspect the best part of your father, as well."

They didn't talk too much about the man whose genes he shared. Sebastian knew very little about him, other than his name and that he'd come into his mother's life at a time when she was at her lowest point. "You're not bitter about his never marrying you, are you?"

No, she wasn't bitter. Just lonely at times. It had passed, but she didn't want the same for her son. "He had a family, a life." Geraldine's smile turned misty as she remembered. "What we had for such a very short while was just something that happened. And how could I be bitter?" She ruffled his hair. "Without him I would have never had you, and you, even when you don't behave the way I want you to, have been an endless source of joy for me." She cleared her throat, signaling an end to the serious discussion. "Now, what's going on between you and Stephanie?"

He gave her the only honest answer he could. "I don't know."

She didn't even hesitate. "Fair enough. See if you can find out. Soon," she added.

Sebastian refused to dwell on the fact that time was their enemy, that it would take this wonderful woman from him and possibly ravage her before it was done with her. Instead, he rose to his feet and saluted. "Yes, ma'am." And then he kissed her cheek.

Leaving his Bedford office at eleven-thirty, Sebastian picked Stephanie up at home. Iris was staying with the twins, although Stephanie had debated bringing them along. She knew Matthew wouldn't mind. But she decided against it. The twins would be distracting and she needed to concentrate on what was being said. It was going to be difficult enough having Sebastian there without adding in the twins. Although, she had to admit she appreciated his offer of support.

Trying to sort things out in her mind, Stephanie remained unusually quiet as they drove to Newport Beach, where Matthew's law firm shared an entire floor with his father's practice. Matthew had three offices. The senior Yarbourough had twelve. Matthew took it all in stride, even though it was a constant reminder to him that whenever he wanted, he could give up his own practice and join the more prestigious one in some capacity.

But he had chosen his lot and was more than content with it. He occupied the offices that he did because the rent was good, due to his father's firm's presence, and the address was impressive to clients. If that meant running into his father on a regular basis, he saw it as a small price to pay.

Everything in life came with a price tag. His skin had long since ceased being thin when it came to matters involving his father.

Matthew welcomed them both into his office, though he looked a little surprised to see Sebastian accompanying Stephanie.

Sebastian read his expression. "I'm here for moral support."

Matthew nodded. There'd obviously been some sort of a truce between them, he thought. Maybe even more, none of which Stephanie had shared with him. That was her prerogative. He didn't exactly make it a point to play true confessions with his sister, either.

"She can always use that." Matthew indicated

two chairs in front of his desk, then rounded it to the other side to face them. He looked at his sister as he took a seat, getting right to it. "I want a list of your friends, Stephanie. As many influential, respected people as you can come up with."

As Stephanie had never been one to maintain a prominent social agenda, this came at her from left field. "Why?"

"We'll need them as character witnesses," Matt told her simply. "People who can testify what an upstanding person you are. Also, people who can tell the judge how Brett felt about his mother and the way she'd treated him while he was growing up."

Stephanie exchanged looks with Sebastian. That sounded an awful lot like mudslinging and she didn't want to resort to that. "Is that really necessary?"

Matthew folded his hands before him on the desk. They were going to need leverage. Janice Collier was a powerful woman accustomed to getting her way. "Every little bit helps."

"But wouldn't that constitute hearsay?" Sebastian asked. They were talking about secondhand testimony at best. He knew enough about the way the law worked to know that this sort of thing wasn't generally admissible in court.

Matthew raised a careless shoulder, then let it fall. "In view of the fact that both Holly and Brett are dead, the evidence might be allowed to be introduced into the record." Leaning forward, he confided to them, "I'm not exactly in my element here, but family court is a great deal less rigid than criminal court. They're more concerned with the welfare of the children involved in these cases, so some rules can be bent a shade." He laughed shortly. "Too bad the old man isn't handling this for you. No one knows more about bending the rules without breaking them than he does."

There was no point in discussing what wasn't going to happen. "I'm perfectly happy with you representing me," Stephanie told her brother firmly.

"Well, you shouldn't be. Not unless you want to lose."

The voice was deep, with its telltale rasp brought on by too many years of smoking. They all turned to see that the door to Matthew's office had not only been opened, but that Carlton Yarbourough was standing in the doorway, the dour expression he reserved for his private life firmly in place.

With small, precise steps that sharply contrasted with the jaunty stride he'd once had, the older man made his way into the room. And in doing so, took command of it, the way he did of everything.

"I don't like losing and I won't," Stephanie said stubbornly, recovering. She looked at her brother. "Matthew will see to that."

The snow-white head shook from side to side as Yarbourough drew closer to the desk.

"The road to hell and good intentions, girl. The road to hell and good intentions," he repeated, barely suppressed impatience in his voice. "Like Matthew said, he doesn't know the first thing about family law. And he doesn't have the killer instinct.'' Clear blue eyes shifted toward Matthew. ''That's the reason he gave me for not coming into the firm, right, boy?''

Matthew remained unruffled. ''We're not here to review my choices, Father.'' He glanced at his watch. ''And I'm a little pressed for time, so—''

''So go, do your errands.'' Yarbourough waved his son away as if he were no more than an annoying inconvenience. ''Go be the shining lackey for the corporate egotists you contracted yourself to. Nobody's stopping you.''

Incensed at her father's flagrant show of disrespect toward her brother, Stephanie stepped in for Matthew when he made no answer to the insults. ''Father, I know you don't think this is important enough to take up anyone's time with, but Matthew's working with me right now. He's helping me retain custody of the twins.''

''No, he's not,'' Yarbourough corrected his daughter. ''But I am.''

For once, her father had rendered her utterly speechless.

Matthew found his tongue first. ''But just last night you said—''

There were few things that Yarbourough liked less than being contradicted. ''I'm the best authority on what I said and didn't say,'' he snapped curtly at his son. "And I'm here, aren't I? Now, go do what you need to do. I'll take over."

"No," Stephanie told him, a quiet edge in her voice. "You won't."

All three men looked at her in varying degrees of stunned disbelief. The least surprised was Sebastian. He knew firsthand how spirited, how stubborn she could be.

It galled her beyond words that her father felt he had the right to play God within the structure of their lives. That he could say no, then for some unknown reason change his mind and come in, commandeering the office, the case and them.

Brows that were no less formidable now that they were nearly white drew together over the bridge of his Roman nose. "Did I hear you right, girl?"

"Yes, you did." She hated the bland term he bandied around, as if she was some sort of eighteenth-century servant meant to wait on him hand and foot. "And I've got a name, Father. It's Stephanie. Say it."

Yarbourough bristled at being talked to this way. "I know what your name is. I'm the one who chose it," he shouted. "I named you after—" Abruptly, he stopped. There was no reason to lapse into an intimate, personal mode. She was his client at the moment, not his daughter. "Never mind who I named you after. Don't be impudent," he warned her.

She was well past being cowed by warnings. "I'll be anything I damn well please. And what gives you the right to just waltz in and play puppet master with everyone's lives, Father?''

Yarbourough's frown deepened with a touch of confusion. ''I thought you'd be pleased.''

''Well, you thought wrong.'' She had to restrain herself to keep from shouting at him. She turned abruptly toward her brother. ''Matthew, I still want you to handle the case.''

''Maybe you'd better rethink that.''

It was Sebastian, not Matthew, who gave her the advice. Stephanie stared at him, dumbfounded. She never would have thought that she'd live to hear Sebastian defend her father.

He'd kept his peace throughout the confrontation, feeling it wasn't his place to say anything. They were family and he was just an outsider. But if it meant sacrificing a victory that would be so precious to her, Sebastian felt he had to say something.

''What is there to rethink?'' she asked, finally finding her tongue. ''My father can't represent me. He's the one who was appalled because I was 'pandering' my body by being a 'baby machine.''' She recalled the exact words that Matthew had said her father had used when he'd found out she was carrying Brett and Holly's babies. They were etched on her heart. ''How is a man like that going to represent me?''

''To the best of his ability,'' Sebastian answered pointedly. His glance passed over Yarbourough. There was no love lost, but he could give the devil his due. In this case, he thought the term rather appropriate. "He doesn't need to believe in you, he just needs to want to win." As far as he knew, winning was everything to Yarbourough. "And we're all aware of your father's track record. There's no doubt that having him in court with you will only help, not hinder your case." He looked at Stephanie pointedly. "The bottom line is getting custody of the twins, isn't it?"

He made her feel ashamed that she'd allowed her feelings to distract her. "Yes."

Sebastian indicated Yarbourough, resting his case. He could see that Matthew agreed with him. For a moment, he felt as if their friendship had regained a little of its old ground. "Then your father's the man to do it."

Yarbourough said nothing, but his sharp features softened a slight degree and there appeared to be a grudging respect in his eyes when he looked at him. Not that it mattered to Sebastian. He could do without the lawyer's respect. That was all moot, anyway. What mattered to him was Stephanie and what she wanted.

Stephanie pressed her lips together. To keep the twins, she was willing to make any compromises. Even to enter into a deal with her father. "All right, if you want to take the case on, we have a deal." Belatedly, she put out her hand.

Her father barely touched it. "Don't worry about the cost, the firm needs a write-off," he assured her, dropping his hand to his side. "I'm taking on the case pro bono."

Only her father would talk to her about money before outlining a single step in the case, she thought bitterly. "No," she told him firmly. "I'll pay you."

He looked as if he thought she'd lost her mind. "Do you realize what you're saying? My services don't come cheaply."

He was one of the highest-paid lawyers in the country, but it wasn't money she was thinking of. "No one knows that better than I do, Father." Well, she'd made her deal, it was time to get it rolling. "Now, what do you need from me?"

Yarbourough looked at his second-born, the daughter he'd never wanted. It was difficult for someone who lived life to the fullest the way he always had to come to terms with the fact that he might not always continue. Immortality was just something he had taken for granted without thought. Something he felt entitled to. Now there was an end to the road, possibly even in sight, and he didn't like it. Didn't like the fact that he might die, *was* dying.

And for some strange reason, along with the knowledge of his pending mortality came the desire to set things right. He'd never been able to abide loose ends, untidiness. The affairs within his private life were chaotic. He'd always managed to get along with his son in some semblance or other, but Stephanie, the child he'd named after his father, Stephan, because no other name had occurred to him, Stephanie was a different matter.

By and large he'd ignored her during her formative years, leaving her upbringing first to her mother, then to a string of nannies and housekeepers. If he thought of her at all, she was an afterthought, nothing more. That had been wrong, he thought, wondering when the hell he'd developed a conscience.

When didn't matter. It was here and he had to deal with it. Yarbourough felt he had to make some sort of amends to Stephanie, some sort of restitution for the years that had been lost, the years he had quite literally ignored her. Winning her the children she refused to get rid of would be that restitution.

"Come into my office and we'll go over this." It wasn't an invitation, it was an order.

Opening the door, Yarbourough was about to walk out, then stopped and stepped to the side, waiting for her to go first. He glanced over his shoulder at Sebastian, who was not far behind.

Grudgingly, he waited for Sebastian to join them. "You, too."

"I was planning to," Sebastian said easily, slipping his hand along her waist.

Stephanie smiled to herself. Nothing in her life was predictable, she decided. Nothing at all, and maybe, just this once, that was a good thing.

* * *

She kept her silence as long as she could. The words were out the minute they stepped into the elevator.

"He's always been horrible to you," Stephanie said, confronting Sebastian as they left her father's office two hours later. "Why did you take his side back there in Matthew's office?"

"I didn't." Sebastian pressed for the ground floor. "I took yours." The ride was swift. No one else got on. "You should always turn to the best, no matter what you're doing. Your father's ego and personality notwithstanding, he is the best."

She laughed as the doors opened and she got off. "You threw him for a loop, you know that, don't you, speaking up for him? You saw that look on his face. He thought that you had lost your mind. Either that, or he had."

His hand on the small of her back, Sebastian guided her in the direction where his car was parked. "That," he told her with a satisfied smile, "was a bonus."

Opening the car door for her, he rounded the hood and got in on the driver's side. No sooner had he strapped himself in and put the key into the ignition than his pager went off. Angling it, he looked down at the number.

"Looks like Mrs. Lopez has gone into labor." The woman was one of several of the newer patients whom Sheila had transferred to him with the patient's consent.

Still a little stunned over what had happened in her brother's law office, it took Stephanie a minute to decide what to do. "I'll go to the hospital with you and get a cab from there." As it was, they were only a short distance away from Harris Memorial.

He didn't like just abandoning Stephanie on such short notice, but there was no question that Mrs. Lopez needed his full attention. This was the woman's first baby and she'd confided to him that she was terrified. He slanted a quick look at her as he drove. "You sure?"

She nodded. "No problem. It's not like I don't know my way around." It wasn't exactly that long ago that she was in Mrs. Lopez's condition. "Tell Mrs. Lopez I'm grateful she waited until after the meeting with my father to go into labor." She hesitated for a moment, then added, "I really needed you in there."

Sebastian glanced at her before looking at the road. He wondered if she realized how much her words meant to him. Probably not.

Chapter Fourteen

The emptiness crept into his subconsciousness, growing until it felt as if it was going to consume him entirely. There was nothing below his feet, nothing above his head. He had only one chance to save himself.

Instincts born of self-preservation had Sebastian reaching to his left. To his lifeline.

To where Stephanie was lying, asleep.

There was nothing.

Sleep and the dream left immediately. Sebastian's eyes opened as the realization sank in: Stephanie wasn't there beside him.

That she had risen in the middle of the night to feed one of the twins was the most logical explanation, but one that never even suggested itself to him. He would have heard the baby cry. He had all the other times since he'd taken to spending nights with Stephanie.

Able to sleep like a rock buried beneath miles of dirt, somehow he had become attuned to the small, high-pitched whimper of each of the twins. He was even beginning to be able to tell them apart by their cry.

It had just happened, he thought, just as his remaining overnight with Stephanie had over these last few weeks. Without conversation, without deliberation. One night he didn't, the next night he did. It was something that had evolved gradually, naturally.

Something both of them, he thought, had taken for granted. She needed his support and he needed her to need him.

So without prior arrangements, one night he had just remained with her. It made logistics a little sticky, but he managed. Mornings he'd leave, stopping in at his mother's, where the rest of his things still hung in the closet. Where his life was supposedly still anchored. He'd check on things with his mother, then go into the office. And looked forward to seeing Stephanie again at the end of the day.

Sebastian told himself that remaining with Stephanie was just a temporary mooring at a harbor, nothing more. Once the custody battle was satisfactorily resolved, once she was emotionally back on her feet, he would naturally go back to his routine and she to hers. But for now, he was here for her.

Except that at the moment, she wasn't here. She'd managed to slip out of bed without waking him. Not an easy matter since he was even more attuned to her than he was to the twins' cries.

Concerned, he sat up. And then he saw her. A small, slender figure standing by the open window, silhouetted by streams of moonlight that sent long, pale yellow fingers through the floor-length nightgown she was wearing. The one he liked that she tended to favor. It was a muted pearl blue, almost entirely see-through and impossibly romantic.

It drove him crazy just to look at her in it.

Desire fisted itself tightly around him, taking him prisoner. He struggled to shake himself free of the passion. It wasn't his desire Stephanie needed, he thought, slipping out of bed.

Sebastian crossed to the window, coming up behind her. Very softly, he placed his hands on her shoulders. He felt her body jolt, stiffening for a second, then relaxing again. Though he could have sworn that there was an underlying layer of tension still there.

Not turning around, Stephanie placed her hand over his on her shoulder and sighed. "I'm sorry, I didn't mean to wake you."

He slipped his arms around her from behind and kissed the top of her head. Damn, but he loved her, he thought. He couldn't remember a moment when he'd loved her more. "Can't sleep?"

There was no point in denying it. Stephanie shook her head. "Too tense." The hearing in family court loomed before her like a merciless ogre. They were due before the judge in the morning. "Too worried."

The embrace around her shoulders tightened. He wished he could make this all go away for her. "You've got a good lawyer."

The irony of the statement, said half in amusement, might have made her laugh at any other time. Because any other time, her stomach wouldn't be so tied up in knots.

"Even so..." Her voice drifted off as she debated saying anything further. But before she could stop the words they were out of her mouth. "I've been thinking of leaving."

He wasn't sure he quite understood. "You mean once the hearing is over?"

She sighed, then turned around in the circle of his arms. He saw the worry etched into her face, saw her red-rimmed eyes. Something in his heart ached. He felt so powerless to help her and the sight of her distress sliced holes all through him.

"No, now. This second. Before the hearing starts." She knew she was talking crazy, but she just wanted to run away, go somewhere where she and her babies would be safe. Somewhere where she wouldn't have to worry about them being taken away from her. "Before they have a chance to take the babies away from me." It could be done. Especially if she hurried. She could be gone more than six hours before they even missed her. "Just pack up what they need and leave."

Hands on his chest in mute supplication, Stephanie searched Sebastian's face, her thoughts running here and there like prey that had been cornered. She hadn't known what she was going to say until the words were out. "Come with me."

He felt the plea go right through him like an arrow, piercing his heart. Stephanie would never know, he thought, what her request meant to him.

He held her to him for a long moment, then kissed her forehead. He didn't believe he'd ever loved her so much as he did right at this moment. "Thanks for the offer, Stevi, but you don't want to do this. Nothing's ever settled by running away."

She drew back from him, amazed. A sense of betrayal filtered through her eyes as she looked up at Sebastian. "How can you say that? That's what you did," she accused him angrily. "You left."

He didn't bother with semantics, with telling her that that was different. That he had left for her own good. They'd been all through that. And maybe, he thought, examining the events all over again, Stephanie was right at that. He shouldn't have left. He should have stayed and talked to her rather than miss his opportunity with her.

A bittersweet smile creased his lips. "Maybe that's how I know it doesn't work." He touched her cheek, caressing it softly. "Nothing is ever settled by leaving, only by staying and facing up to it. Otherwise, it haunts you for the rest of your life." The way leaving Bedford and Stephanie had haunted him. His mouth curved. "Besides, the Stephanie Yarbourough I know doesn't turn tail and run. She's not a quitter."

Oh, yes, she was, Stephanie thought, suddenly incredibly weary and drained. "Maybe she's tired of taking on the world."

With his finger beneath her chin, he lifted her head until her eyes were level with his. "She doesn't have to take it on alone."

She appreciated the gesture, but that didn't change what she was ultimately afraid of happening. "But if I lose—"

"We'll appeal," he promised. "And continue to appeal until you finally win." He smiled into her eyes, trying to infuse her with the confidence he felt. "Besides, you won't lose."

She laughed shortly, moving away from him. Pacing, she ran her hands up and down her arms to ward off a chill that went down clear to her bones. "Why, because my father decided to atone for all his past sins and get in my corner?"

"There's that," he conceded, but he was thinking more along the lines of appealing to Brett's mother. "And maybe there's a way to get to Brett's mother. Appeal to her softer nature."

"Ha," she laughed harshly, recalling the stories of

neglect, of name-calling and abuse that had been passed on to her through Holly. "Barracudas don't have a softer nature."

"Maybe mother barracudas do." Taking her hand, he slowly drew her back to the bed, then coaxed her to lie down. "Now, get back into bed and get some rest." He covered her with the comforter, then rounded the bed to his own side and got in. "You don't want to go to court looking as if you spend your nights carousing." He slid her to him, folding his arm around her and holding her close. "It's going to be all right. I promise."

She knew it was utterly ridiculous to gather comfort from his words. There was no way he could promise her something like that. But somehow, hearing him say it made her believe that it could be so. With a sigh, she snuggled against him and tried to find a few more hours of sleep before dawn.

Stephanie caught her breath, pressing her lips together so hard she thought they would start to bleed. What she really wanted to do was leap to her feet and tell the smug-looking woman sitting at the other table in the small courtroom exactly what she thought of her. But shouting words like that wouldn't help her retain custody of the twins. It would only work against her, so she kept her peace.

But it was far from easy.

The lawyer Janice Collier had hired to gain her custody of her grandchildren stood at their table, holding aloft a folder of photographs as if he'd scored damning evidence that would swing the entire matter to his client's favor. He swished the folder through the air like a fatal sword.

"They say a picture is worth a thousand words, Your Honor." In case the presiding judge had missed the folder, he waved it with a flourish. "I have here, then, ten thousand words." The tall, immaculately dressed man smiled thinly. "Ten thousand words to prove that this young woman is an unfit mother." It was clear that he wanted to approach the bench, but was restraining himself. "She's attempting to secure custody of Brett Collier's children, yet she neglects these same helpless infants in order to spend her nights in the embrace of a man she has only recently taken up with." The attorney looked properly aghast. "This isn't the kind of morality Mrs. Collier or any decent woman would want her grandchildren subjected to."

The gray-haired woman sitting on the bench looked at the attorney peevishly. "No grandstanding, please, Mr. Alder. The court readily understands what you're trying to imply."

"If I may approach the bench and place these into evidence," Alder requested submissively.

Stephanie felt her stomach tighten another notch and her temper rise up two.

"You may." Judge Anderson beckoned him forward. The attorney lost no time in setting the folder on the bar, then returning to his place in the court-room.

Seated at the table for moral support and acting in conjunction with his father, Matthew began to rise to say something in Stephanie's defense. Yarbourough stopped him with a look, then placed both hands on the table and rose to his feet. Only Stephanie noticed how heavily he leaned on the palms of his hands in order to get up.

Like fine classical music, his deep, resonant voice filled the courtroom. "Your Honor, if I may speak. Whom Ms. Yarbourough chooses to spend her time with does not influence the care she's giving to the infants—"

"What care?" Alder demanded contemptuously, dramatically pulling the proverbial gloves off. "How can she hear them if she's off in another room, toasting her sheets with that man?" Turning slightly to his right, Alder indicated Sebastian sitting behind Stephanie.

Stephanie saw a hint of color creep up along her father's neck. She knew that it galled him to be placed in a position where he had to defend not only her seeing Sebastian, but Sebastian, as well.

"That man," said Yarbourough, with a calm voice that belied his inner feelings, "is a doctor. The doctor, as it turns out, who delivered the twins." He allowed himself a slight, confident smile. "Who better to have available around infants than a doctor?" The superior expression intensified as he looked to-

ward the opposing counsel. "In addition, this isn't
the tawdry affair my learned colleague is so desperately attempting to allude to. Dr. Sebastian Caine is
an old friend of Ms. Yarbourough's. They grew up
together and there was talk of marriage between them
several years ago."

He grasped the ends of his lapels, a habit he fa-
vored whenever he was feeling particularly confident. Stephanie thought of it as his Clarence Darrow
pose. He was a man at complete ease in his element.

"But we aren't here to discuss old friendships being renewed. We are here to decide the welfare of
two infants." He slanted a long glance toward Alder.
"Two infants who would profit from a mother's love.
The kind of love that comes from the bond of feeling
forged when their hearts beat beneath hers." His
voice rose just a touch, heavy with emotion. "The
kind of bond that comes from carrying them for nine
months, of being part of them and they part of her."

Alder sneered, rising to his feet, as well, as if that
was the only way to capture the judge's attention.

"Very touching, but just because one person might
carry around the luggage belonging to a friend for a
number of days or weeks or months," he added significantly, contempt obvious in his voice, "that
doesn't make the luggage theirs. By law, the luggage
still belongs to that friend, and, should that friend no
longer be able to claim their luggage, it belongs to
the friend's next of kin." Pale brown eyes swept the

courtroom, resting on Stephanie. "I believe we're all agreed on that."

The triumph was evident on her father's face, even though Stephanie felt far from confident herself. "Are you referring to the infants as luggage, Mr. Alder?"

The other attorney blustered, but only slightly. "No, I am using a metaphor to make a point. Ms. Yarbourough entered into a lawfully executed contract to bear these infants for Brett and Holly Collier. The children have the Colliers' DNA, not hers. Since neither Mr. or Mrs. Collier are alive to claim those babies, who are the natural exponent of this lawful contract, we can only conclude that Brett Collier's mother, Janice Collier, has a lawful right, not to mention a moral one, to take custody of her grandchildren immediately."

Distraught, unable to sit quietly by as the verbal Ping-Pong match went on around her, Stephanie finally spoke up.

"She can't love them the way I do." She ignored the silencing glare her father sent her way. "Your Honor, on her deathbed Holly Collier begged me not to let her mother-in-law have the babies. She repeated what I already knew firsthand, that Brett had confided in her that his childhood was a miserable one fraught with neglect and verbal abuse. He didn't want that for his babies. I made Holly a deathbed promise that I would keep them myself, no matter what."

"All very touching," Alder said dismissively, "but nonetheless, mere hearsay on top of hearsay, Your Honor." He shook his head. "We have only Ms. Yarbourough's word for what was said—"

The judge held her hand up to silence the attorney before he could unfurl his tongue and become carried away with rhetoric again.

"I'm well aware of the definition of hearsay, Mr. Alder." She opened the folder and frowned, then raised her eyes toward Stephanie. "I'm afraid I'm going to need some time to look over the photographs and the accompanying report Mr. Alder was kind enough to include. Obviously Mr. Alder feels the court needs help in analyzing the photographs." She closed the folder and slid it to the side of the bar. "Court's adjourned until tomorrow morning at nine."

As the gavel resounded, punctuating the statement, Stephanie felt as if it had slammed down on her chest as well. Gathering her things together, she turned and saw that Sebastian wasn't sitting behind her any longer, but had retreated to the rear of the courtroom. He was talking to Matthew, who was taking in what was being said in thoughtful silence.

Her legs felt numb as she rose to her feet. Like a preprogrammed robot, she began to walk toward her brother and Sebastian, only vaguely wondering what they were discussing. Her mind was far too full of abysmal scenarios to really speculate about what had brought Sebastian and his former best friend together.

The hand on her shoulder momentarily kept her from finding out.

When she turned she found herself looking at her father's condemning expression. "You realize that this would have been a lot simpler if you hadn't gotten involved with him."

His question struck her as so ironic, she struggled not to laugh. The sound would have undoubtedly been hysterical and done her little good.

"It would have been simpler if you hadn't made him leave town in the first place," she pointed out. "But that's in the past and there's no changing it...."

He didn't bother arguing with her. Always expedient, he moved on. "If you'd like, I can see if I can get that pompous ass, Alder, to talk to Collier and see if I can arrange visitation rights for you."

An icy hand passed over her heart, but she kept her expression sober as she looked at her father. "So you're giving up?"

"No one's giving up," he informed her tersely. "But I am being a realist and covering all bases." He scrutinized her. "Do you really want to continue and have our name raked over the coals?"

How could he even ask such a question? "*Yes,* I want to continue. I want to do anything that's necessary to win this case. And I don't give a damn about raking our name over the coals, Father. You should know that by now.'' She slung her purse strap over her shoulder. ''This is the twenty-first century, not the Dark Ages, or haven't you heard? They don't stone people for finding comfort in each other's arms anymore.''

Yarbourough blew out a breath, his long fingers drumming impatiently on the long tabletop. Then, placing his papers in his briefcase and snapping it shut, he glanced toward the other table where Mrs. Collier and her lawyer were still conferring.

''All right, have it your way. I'll see you back here at ten of nine tomorrow morning.''

''I'll be here.''

Stephanie turned toward where Sebastian was still standing with her brother. Curiosity nudged its way into the foreground as she got a grip on her thoughts. Sebastian had been at her side throughout the proceedings these last two days. Though ever since she could remember she'd prided herself on being an independent person who didn't need anyone, in her heart she knew that she would have been perilously close to coming unraveled without Sebastian there to give her silent support. She owed him a great deal. More than she could ever hope to say.

As she approached the two men, she saw Matthew look her way, nod at Sebastian while he shook his hand, and then leave the courtroom. He didn't say a word to her, which she thought was odd.

''What was all that about?'' she asked Sebastian as she joined him.

Sebastian glanced toward the closing courtroom door. "I was just asking Matthew some legal advice."

That illuminated nothing. "About?"

Sebastian watched as Yarbourough walked past him. Not a single glance came his way. "What he thought chances of winning this case were."

She could feel her nerves tightening. It was getting increasingly more difficult to hold on to her control. "He said good, I hope, because Matthew is a born optimist, and if he said bad, then I know we're in trouble."

Her words were falling out one on top of another. He knew her. Stephanie always talked quickly whenever she was really nervous. Mentally, he crossed his fingers as he continued.

"Well, I didn't exactly ask about chances," Sebastian corrected her.

He looked around the courtroom. Mrs. Collier and her attorney had left, along with the judge and the bailiff. Only the court stenographer still remained, gathering her notes and her machine together. This wasn't the kind of atmosphere he would have chosen to say these words to her. But desperate times begat desperate actions. His hands on her shoulders, he moved her toward a corner of the courtroom so even if the stenographer passed them, she wouldn't be able to hear what was being said.

"I asked Matthew if you'd stand a better chance

getting custody of the twins if you were married, and he said yes, you would.''

Her eyes narrowed as she looked at him. ''But I'm not married—''

''Yet.'' Sebastian looked into her eyes. She looked afraid, he thought. He didn't want her to be. ''Stephanie, will you marry me?''

Chapter Fifteen

Stephanie stared at him in numbed, disbelieving silence. "What is this, a joke?"

"No, I'm asking you to marry me." He couldn't begin to understand why she looked so upset with him. "Will you marry me?" Sebastian repeated when she said nothing.

Slowly, the numbness receded. To be replaced by anger. This wasn't a real proposal. At best it was one born of necessity, and in voicing it, he'd robbed her of something precious. He'd tarnished the memory of what had once been. When he'd asked her the first time. When he'd meant it.

"No," she said firmly, her hands clenched at her sides. "My answer is no. No, I won't marry you."

In the distance, the door closed behind the stenographer as she retreated. The silence surrounded the single word of refusal Stephanie had uttered, magnifying it.

For a moment, in the face of her anger and rejection, Sebastian didn't know what to say, how to react. Self-preservation would have had him withdrawing. But this wasn't about self-preservation, it was about Stephanie. Stephanie and the children she was struggling to keep as part of her life. She'd already lost one, he owed it to her to help her keep these.

Trying hard to restrain his own temper, he grabbed her by the arm as she turned from him and forced her to look at him.

"Why?"

Her eyes blazed as curt, cutting words fought to emerge from her mouth. She wanted to call him hurtful names, to scream at him for being so cruel, so cold as to destroy the last fragments of the only illusion she had left.

She squared her shoulders as she faced him. "I could ask you the same thing. Why? Why now, why not before? *Any* time before?"

There was no easy, two-or three-word answer to that. It wasn't as if the proposal, the thought, had ever been far from his mind. But he knew it wouldn't have been right to have asked her then. Too much time had passed, there was too much in the way. But the custody battle had pushed all that aside.

"What does it matter? I'm asking now."

Part of her just wanted to run from him. To hurry home to some dark place and just curl up and cry until there was nothing left within her. But the part of her that had always fought battles, that had stood up for herself, wanted him to know what he and his proposal had just done to her heart.

"Oh, it matters all right. It matters a lot. Because if you'd wanted just me, then you would have asked before. You would have never left, or if you actually believed you left for noble purposes, you would have come to your senses and returned." It was difficult keeping her voice down as emotion spiked through it. "Or you would have wanted me so badly that noble intentions wouldn't have messed up your thinking."

Somehow, she managed to pull herself together. The look in her eyes told him to go to hell.

"But you didn't come back to me, you didn't ask me to marry you then, and I won't live the rest of my life knowing that you asked me to marry you out of pity, or guilt or some other godforsaken noble sacrifice on your part." His pager suddenly went off, its sound mocking the words that were being said. Sebastian ignored it. Stephanie pulled away as he reached for her again and pushed the heavy black door open with the flat of her hand. "Now, leave me alone." The pager went off again, sounding almost insistent. "Go, go answer your pager and *leave me alone!*" she shouted as she ran off.

The sound of her heels clicking on the marble floor echoed in his brain.

His mouth felt like cotton. Torn between following her and answering the page that had come in, Sebastian wavered for a moment. His sense of obligation won out and he looked down at the number on his pager.

But damn, he wanted to go after her.

Maybe she needed some time alone, he told himself. And maybe he did, too.

Swallowing a curse, Sebastian took out his cell phone and punched in the numbers that were highlighted on his pager.

Exhausted, Sebastian took off the surgical mask that hung precariously around his neck like a wilting lover that still refused to withdraw her arms. He looked at his watch.

Ten past ten.

It felt as if it should be a lot later than that. He'd had not one delivery to contend with but two. Two deliveries that had managed to practically dovetail into each other, overlapping by some ten or fifteen minutes. He'd no sooner cut the umbilical cord from Mrs. Witwer's son than his answering service alerted him to the fact that Mrs. Grossman and her husband were on their way to the hospital posthaste.

Scrubbing his hand over his face, Sebastian went to the tiny room off the nurses' station that served as a doctors' lounge without even bothering to change his clothes. He wanted to call Stephanie, to see how she was doing. All through the deliveries the sight of Stephanie's angry eyes had haunted him.

The lounge was empty. He crossed to the small side table and sat down. But as he raised the receiver to his ear and began to dial Stephanie's number, he changed his mind. He let the receiver drop back into the cradle. Sebastian rose to his feet again.

This wasn't something he could say to her over the telephone. But it wasn't something he could back away from, either, the way she'd all but ordered him to. As he hurried over to the locker room and his locker, the wheels in his head began to turn.

He needed to make a stop somewhere before he went to see Stephanie.

Getting back into his car an hour later, Sebastian drove straight to Stephanie's house. He still had no idea what he was going to say to her. No idea how to smooth this over and make it right. For both of them.

His mother had once counseled him that when he was at a loss for words, to open up his heart and see what poured out. He figured that maybe his mother had the right idea. Especially since nothing else occurred to him.

Nerves haunted her every move as Stephanie tried to occupy herself with the thousand and one things that went into caring for twins. Fielding Iris's questions as best she could, she'd sent the woman home shortly after she'd returned from family court. Feeling incredibly drained, she still wanted to spend as much time with the twins as possible. Like a dry sponge, she soaked up every second, every detail.

The worst-case scenario continued to hover in Stephanie's mind like a ghoulish specter, refusing to retreat no matter what logic she tried to use in order to vanquish it.

What if she woke up some morning and the twins weren't there any longer? What would she do with herself? How would she go on? The two infants had come to mean so much to her so quickly.

As had Sebastian, she thought sadly, cuddling Holly to her breast and moving slowly back and forth in the rocking chair Matthew had given her. But she'd ended it today. There was no other way to look at it. She'd ordered him out of her life and he'd gone.

She smiled down at the drowsy face, her heart quickening with so much love she could hardly breathe. It helped having this small being in her arms, helped to mute the hurt she felt at what had happened between her and Sebastian. For her to dwell on what might have been had she accepted his sudden marriage proposal was just stupid. She hadn't accepted, even though a part of her had desperately wanted to, wanted him at any price, under any pretext.

But she knew that eventually she'd hate herself for being so needy, hate him for not loving her enough to make all of this unnecessary. For not having asked her before all this had come up so that she wouldn't have been riddled with doubts about his feelings.

She sighed and the baby stirred against her, the long black lashes flickering slightly before lowering again, dark crescents against rose-petal-soft cheeks.

The doorbell rang just then. Stephanie looked off in the general direction of the front of the house wearily. More than likely, it was her father, here to plot strategy. She could remember hearing him return home at two in the morning when she was growing up, wired because he'd found the key to winning some case.

She wasn't up to seeing him. Stephanie rose to her feet slowly.

"Time to go to bed, sugar," she murmured, placing Holly back in her crib. She slipped the cotton blanket over the small form. "Be a good girl and don't wake up your brother, okay?"

Stephanie blinked back tears, holding a tight rein on her thoughts. Two drops escaped, anyway. She wiped them away with her fingers before going downstairs.

Opening the door, she stopped dead when she saw him. Expecting to see the thin, bent frame that now belonged to her father, finding Sebastian on her doorstep took her aback.

Stupid to have her heart leap up that way at the sight of him. When was she going to learn?

Her fingers tightened on the doorknob as she

stood, blocking his entry. "Is this a pity visit?" Her voice was strained, cold.

It was going to be an uphill battle, but he'd already fought one tonight. This one should be easier. He looked down into her unsmiling face.

"Can I come in?"

She didn't move. "I don't see the need. Nothing's changed, especially not my mind. I'm going to win custody of these children without resorting to any kind of trickery, and that includes marrying someone under false pretenses."

She looked tired beneath that bravado of hers, he thought. Very gently, he placed his hands on her shoulders and moved her out of the way, then walked in.

"There are no false pretenses and there's no trickery involved, Stevi."

Still standing in the foyer, she gave up and closed the door, then followed him into the living room. "What do you call proposing to me?"

He turned around to look at her. "Hopeful," he answered. Taking her hands in his, he drew her onto the sofa and sat down with her. "Stevi, when I left Bedford and you, it was for what I felt was a noble reason. But noble or not, I knew then—and now—that I'd left my soul behind."

He saw the resistance in her eyes. She didn't want to believe him, didn't want to let herself believe him. He knew how she thought. Knew everything about her. He had to convince her.

"I haven't been able to find it since. Not in my life, not in my work. Not until I came back and looked into your eyes. That's where my soul is, Stevi. Trapped in your eyes." He brought her hands up to his lips and kissed each one in turn, then continued holding them as he spoke. "Because the first time you looked at me, you took it away. I'll never be whole without you, Stevi. If marrying you helps you make a case for keeping the twins, that's just a bonus and I'm glad of it. But that's not why I'm asking you to marry me.

"I'm asking because I can't hold out any longer. I'm asking because I love you and will love you until the day I die no matter what you tell me. But I'm only going to accept your refusal if you can look at me and tell me that you don't feel the same way I do. That you don't love me. Say it and I'll go away and won't bother you anymore."

Her heart pounding madly, Stephanie blew out a shaky breath.

"Oh, I can say it, all right." She pressed her lips together as she looked into his eyes. "But I can't mean it. It wouldn't be true and you know it." She cocked her head, looking at him. "You've always known everything there was to know about me." She smiled ruefully. "Sometimes even before I knew it."

"Then you'll marry me?"

She bit her lip to keep the smile from splitting her face. "Well, if you're absolutely sure that it's not because of the twins, or because you feel guilty about leaving me in the first place—''

"Shut up, Stevi, you talk too much." His lips covered hers, curtailing any further dialogue for a long, long time.

Later that night, as she lay in bed beside him, spent and content, Stephanie curled into his body, her head cradled against his chest.

"We have to tell my father—'' She was thinking of the hearing and how it might affect the proceedings.

He smiled to himself, thinking of how he'd gotten firsthand knowledge of where the term "bearding the lion in his den" had originated. "I already did."

She raised herself up on her elbow to look at him. "When?"

"Right after I delivered Mrs. Grossman's bouncing baby boy." Raising his head slightly, he pressed a kiss to her temple and drew her closer to him. "I left the hospital and drove over to see your father."

Amazed, Stephanie sat up and looked at him. The sheet pooled around her waist. "He talked to you?"

Propping himself up on his elbow, Sebastian entertained himself by passing his hand lightly over her breasts. He could feel desire resurging in his veins, tightening his loins.

"He wasn't happy about it at first, but I got him to listen." He liked the way her nipples hardened against the palm of his hand as he gently rubbed them. "And to grudgingly agree that if I married you, you'd have a stronger case for providing a stable home for the twins. It also puts our 'affair' in a better light." He grinned at her. "Makes those photographs of Alder's null and void, in a way."

He was fogging her brain. She struggled to pay attention. "Then my father thinks that you're marrying me so that I can retain custody…?"

He wasn't about to get into that quagmire again. "No, I made it clear to him that I was still in love with you and that I thought I was an ass for listening to him years ago." Sebastian shook his head as he laughed. Wonders, it seemed, had never ceased. "He actually agreed with me."

"My father?" That didn't seem possible. But then, Sebastian could always accomplish the impossible. "Are you sure you were at the right house?"

He turned her toward him, fitting her over his torso so that she straddled him. "I checked the mailbox before I left. Had his name on it." Very lightly, he began to knead her thighs. "He was on the phone with the opposing counsel when I left. We're all meeting tomorrow morning before court's in session."

She knew she should take some kind of offense, but for the life of her, she just couldn't muster up the indignation. She was far too happy. Still, she couldn't let him get away with it completely. "But you did all this presupposing I'd say yes. What if I'd turned you down again?"

He feathered his fingers through her hair, framing her face. "The advantage of having my soul trapped within your eyes, Stevi, is that I get a hint of what you're feeling, as well. I had a feeling that you still loved me. I just had to make you realize it."

She laughed, leaning over him and nipping his lower lip between her teeth. She ran her tongue over it and felt him move beneath her.

"Pretty cocky, aren't you?"

He brought her mouth back to his. "Only about some things, Stevi. Only about some things."

Stephanie realized she was gripping his hand too tightly. Tension had her squeezing Sebastian's fingers hard. They were in an empty judge's chambers, facing Brett's mother and her attorney over an oak table. Her heart hadn't left her throat since she, Sebastian and her father and brother had walked into the room.

There was so much riding on this.

Everything that both Brett and Holly had told her had convinced her that his mother was devoid of any maternal feelings. That family pride was the only reason Janice Collier was even pursuing custody of her grandchildren. That, she thought, gave the woman a great deal in common with her father.

Yet the appeal she was verbally making right now was being made to a grandmother, not a matriarch without a family to oversee. Even as she spoke,

Stephanie had to admit to herself that her hopes for success weren't very high.

Janice Collier sat and listened quietly, a regal frown on her face, her expression removed. It was as if the words were not even entering her ears but were merely producing buzzing noises that passed by without creating any sort of an impression whatsoever.

Stephanie felt like taking the woman and shaking her by the shoulders, making her listen. Making her agree to cease in her pursuit of custody of the twins.

Finished, Stephanie sat back in her chair.

And then her father rose and asked permission to speak to Janice in private.

The woman looked at him coldly before nodding at the man to her right. "Anything you say to me will have to be said in front of my lawyer."

"All right, if those are your wishes," Yarbourough conceded. "Mrs. Collier, you and I have far more in common than prominent positions on a social register. We can both be referred to as feelingless, pompous asses."

Sebastian pressed his lips together to keep a smile from emerging. Stephanie's father was quoting what he had said to him at one point last night verbatim.

Alder jumped to his feet. "Mr. Yarbourough—"

Her face a subdued shade of crimson, Janice Collier placed a restraining hand on her lawyer's, holding him in place. The man reluctantly took his seat beside her. Mrs. Collier's icy eyes remained fixed on the man standing in front of her. "Go on."

"We've both become so enamored with the sound of our last names, with the importance attached to our positions, that we've forgotten that we're merely mortals, not icons." An ironic half smile played on his lips as he uttered the word *mortals*. "And mortals, it turns out, need certain things. They need peace. They need the knowledge that, when necessary, they can turn to someone not for dispassionate advice, but for just comfort. Warmth." He looked at his daughter before continuing. "The knowledge that at the end of the road, someone will mourn them, not because an institution has passed away, or an icon, but a human being who meant something to them."

Fleetingly, his eyes touched Sebastian's with a grudging respect that surprised both himself and, he could see, to a lesser degree, the recipient. He'd always been someone who gave men their due, and Caine had showed a great deal of nerve and courage by coming to see him last night. By confronting him and making him see the proverbial light—or at least a glimmer of it.

"If you take these children away from my daughter, what can you possibly give them in return to make up for it? They would interfere with your way of life and, ultimately, be raised as the veritable orphans they are. You would grow to resent them and they you. However—" he turned toward Stephanie

"—if you allow my daughter to retain custody of them, she and her husband would allow you to sweep into their lives whenever you felt the desire to do so." He knew Alder had informed the woman of Stephanie's pending marriage to Sebastian. This time, the smile that played on Yarbourough's lips was a genuine one, born of anticipation. With his doctor telling him yesterday that his cancer might be going into remission, he might even see his grandchildren grow up. "I'm told that is the best part of being a grandparent.

"The children would grow to love you rather than resent you. This would be a chance for you to do something good and noble—and earn the love of two very small, important people." He looked at the woman pointedly. "Your legacy is in your own hands, Mrs. Collier. Think very carefully how you want to be remembered."

She pressed her lips together, then withdrew to the rear of the room to confer with her lawyer behind a delicate, ring-bejeweled hand. Stephanie rose and kissed her father's cheek, completely surprising him.

"Thank you," she murmured. "I had no idea you had that in you."

He laughed shortly, but his eyes were no longer cold, no longer distant.

"Neither did I." And, until he had said the words, he hadn't realized how much he actually believed them. "I suppose the old adage is true. You're never too old to learn."

Alder returned to the table, clearing his throat. "All right," he began. "Mrs. Collier has agreed to withdraw her suit as long as she has complete access to visit the twins."

"That was never an issue," Stephanie said. "She's their grandmother. Why shouldn't she be able to see them whenever she wants?" Rounding the table to Mrs. Collier's side, Stephanie stood next to the woman and put out her hand. "Truce."

After a moment, Janice Collier took the hand that was offered and shook it. "Truce," she murmured stiffly.

Sebastian was the first one at Stephanie's side. He caught her by the waist and held her up high, spinning her once around before putting her back down again. "Glad that's out of the way. Now we can start planning our wedding and the rest of our lives. I don't know about you, but I can hardly wait."

"You *are* the rest of my life," Stephanie told him, her eyes misting over. She had a very strong feeling that some of the words she'd heard her father utter today, the words that had moved her and had won her the twins, had been because of him.

Just as he lowered his mouth to hers, oblivious to the fact that the others were still present in the room with them, Sebastian's pager went off. He ignored it.

"That's your pager," Stephanie told him when he made no move to look at the number.

"It's going to have to wait for a minute." He drew her closer. "Until after I kiss my future wife."

It was a long minute.

* * * * *

Don't forget to look out for
the next exciting story in Marie's
CHILDFINDERS, INC. series.
HEART OF A HERO (IM #1105)
will be available next month!

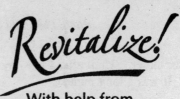

SILHOUETTE® MAKES YOU A STAR!

Feel like a star with Silhouette.

We will fly you and a guest to New York City for an exciting weekend stay at a glamorous 5-star hotel. Experience a refreshing day at one of New York's trendiest spas and have your photo taken by a professional. Plus, receive $1,000 U.S. spending money!

Flowers...long walks...dinner for two... how does Silhouette Books make romance come alive for you?

Send us a script, with 500 words or less, along with visuals (only drawings, magazine cutouts or photographs or combination thereof). Show us how Silhouette Makes Your Love Come Alive. Be creative and have fun. No purchase necessary. All entries must be clearly marked with your name, address and telephone number. All entries will become property of Silhouette and are not returnable. **Contest closes September 28, 2001.**

Please send your entry to: **Silhouette Makes You a Star!**

In U.S.A.	In Canada
P.O. Box 9069	P.O. Box 637
Buffalo, NY, 14269-9069	Fort Erie, ON, L2A 5X3

Look for contest details on the next page, by visiting www.eHarlequin.com or request a copy by sending a self-addressed envelope to the applicable address above. Contest open to Canadian and U.S. residents who are 18 or over. Void where prohibited.

Silhouette®
Where love comes alive™

Our lucky winner's photo will appear in a Silhouette ad. Join the fun!

SRMYAS1

HARLEQUIN "SILHOUETTE MAKES YOU A STAR!" CONTEST 1308
OFFICIAL RULES
NO PURCHASE NECESSARY TO ENTER

1. To enter, follow directions published in the offer to which you are responding. Contest begins June 1, 2001, and ends on September 28, 2001. Entries must be postmarked by September 28, 2001, and received by October 5, 2001. Enter by hand-printing (or typing) on an 8 ½" x 11" piece of paper your name, address (including zip code), contest number/name and attaching a script containing <u>500 words or less, along with drawings, photographs or magazine cutouts, or combinations thereof</u> (i.e., collage) <u>on no larger than 9" x 12"</u> piece of paper, describing how the <u>Silhouette books make romance come alive for you</u>. Mail via first-class mail to: Harlequin "Silhouette Makes You a Star!" Contest 1308, (in the U.S.) P.O. Box 9069, Buffalo, NY 14269-9069, (in Canada) P.O. Box 637, Fort Erie, Ontario, Canada L2A 5X3. Limit one entry per person, household or organization.

2. Contests will be judged by a panel of members of the Harlequin editorial, marketing and public relations staff. Fifty percent of criteria will be judged against script and fifty percent will be judged against drawing, photographs and/or magazine cutouts. Judging criteria will be based on the following:

   - Sincerity—25%
   - Originality and Creativity—50%
   - Emotionally Compelling—25%

   In the event of a tie, duplicate prizes will be awarded. Decisions of the judges are final.

3. All entries become the property of Torstar Corp. and may be used for future promotional purposes. Entries will not be returned. No responsibility is assumed for lost, late, illegible, incomplete, inaccurate, nondelivered or misdirected mail.

4. Contest open only to residents of the U.S. (<u>except Puerto Rico</u>) and Canada who are 18 years of age or older, and is void wherever prohibited by law; all applicable laws and regulations apply. Any litigation within the Province of Quebec respecting the conduct or organization of a publicity contest may be submitted to the Régie des alcools, des courses et des jeux for a ruling. Any litigation respecting the awarding of a prize may be submitted to the Régie des alcools, des courses et des jeux only for the purpose of helping the parties reach a settlement. Employees and immediate family members of Torstar Corp. and D. L. Blair, Inc., their affiliates, subsidiaries and all other agencies, entities and persons connected with the use, marketing or conduct of this contest are not eligible to enter. Taxes on prizes are the sole responsibility of the winner. Acceptance of any prize offered constitutes permission to use winner's name, photograph or other likeness for the purposes of advertising, trade and promotion on behalf of Torstar Corp., its affiliates and subsidiaries without further compensation to the winner, unless prohibited by law.

5. Winner will be determined no later than November 30, 2001, and will be notified by mail. Winner will be required to sign and return an Affidavit of Eligibility/Release of Liability/Publicity Release form within 15 days after winner notification. Noncompliance within that time period may result in disqualification and an alternative winner may be selected. All travelers must execute a Release of Liability prior to ticketing and must possess required travel documents (e.g., passport, photo ID) where applicable. Trip must be booked by December 31, 2001, and completed within one year of notification. No substitution of prize permitted by winner. Torstar Corp. and D. L. Blair, Inc., their parents, affiliates and subsidiaries are not responsible for errors in printing of contest, entries and/or game pieces. In the event of printing or other errors that may result in unintended prize values or duplication of prizes, all affected game pieces or entries shall be null and void. **Purchase or acceptance of a product offer does not improve your chances of winning.**

6. Prizes: (1) Grand Prize—A 2-night/3-day trip for two (2) to New York City, including round-trip coach air transportation nearest winner's home and hotel accommodations (double occupancy) at The Plaza Hotel, a glamorous afternoon makeover at <u>a trendy New York spa</u>, $1,000 in U.S. spending money and an opportunity to <u>have a professional photo taken and appear in a Silhouette advertisement</u> (approximate retail value: $7,000). (10) Ten Runner-Up Prizes of gift packages (retail value $50 ea.). Prizes consist of only those items listed as part of the prize. Limit one prize per person. Prize is valued in U.S. currency.

7. For the name of the winner (available after December 31, 2001) send a self-addressed, stamped envelope to: Harlequin "Silhouette Makes You a Star!" Contest 1197 Winners, P.O. Box 4200 Blair, NE 68009-4200 or you may access the www.eHarlequin.com Web site through February 28, 2002.

Contest sponsored by Torstar Corp., P.O Box 9042, Buffalo, NY 14269-9042.

SRMYAS2

COMING NEXT MONTH

SPECIAL EDITION

#1423 THE MARRIAGE CONSPIRACY—Christine Rimmer
Conveniently Yours
Single mom Joleen Tilly married her best friend, Dekker Smith—
aka Russell Bravo—heir to the Bravo fortune, strictly to keep
custody of her son. But once under the same roof, this couple found
it impossible to sleep in separate beds. Now Dekker must decide if
his heart, once destroyed by love, could ever heal again....

#1424 DATELINE MATRIMONY—Gina Wilkins
Hot Off the Press
Each morning waitress Teresa Scott served breakfast to reporter
Riley O'Neal, but he wanted more than a refill of coffee—*he wanted
her.* A working woman with responsibilities, she had no time for no-
strings fun. Then a scandalous news story had them teaming up
together and hoping that it would end happily ever after....

#1425 THE TRUTH ABOUT TATE—Marilyn Pappano
Tate Rawlins would do anything to protect his family. So when
journalist Natalie Grant threatened to expose his illegitimate half
brother, the rancher took on his brother's identity. But when he fell
in love with the enemy, was the only thing that stood between them
the truth about Tate?

#1426 HIS LITTLE GIRL'S LAUGHTER—Karen Rose Smith
Rafe Pierson's little girl hadn't uttered a word since her mother's death,
so the devoted single father sought out psychologist Shannon Collins
for help. But when the lovely doctor turned his daughter's frown into
laughter once more, would Rafe realize that he also needed
Shannon...for a lifetime?

#1427 THE WOMAN FOR DUSTY CONRAD—Tori Carrington
Dusty was back in town to get a divorce from his former wife, feisty
firefighter Jolie Conrad...whom he'd once believed was the only
woman for him. But when a fire flared, he was right by Jolie's side.
Would this long-burning blaze become the torch that lit their way into
each other's arms again?

#1428 COWGIRL BE MINE—Elaine Nichols
A Woman's Way
Ten years ago, cowgirl Mandy Thomson trampled Jake Miller's
heart. Now she was faced with the painful aftermath of a devastating
bull riding accident. But when she found herself living under the
same roof as Jake, could he heal her wounded pride, and she—her
lover's heart?